Brandon: Encouraged to Dream

The Barnabas Chronicles Book. 7

By

Ronna M. Bacon

Jeremiah 29:11
For I know the thoughts that I think toward you, says the Lord, thoughts of peace and not of evil, to give you a future and a hope.
NKJV

Table of Contents

Chapter 1

Hands tucked in the pockets of his jean jacket, jacket collar turned up just because, a baseball cap tugged down over his mahogany-coloured hair, Brandon Conaghan sniffed the air appreciatively. The scent of hamburgers, hot dogs, peameal bacon, chips, cotton candy and caramel corn wafted through the late summer/early autumn air to tickle at his nose. He smiled. It was definitely the right day to be out and about and to wend his way through the arts and crafts fair. His blue eyes that reminded people of the deep blue of a summer's day assessed the area, his mind wandering to where he should go first.

Brandon sighed to himself as he tugged at the brim of his cap. He wasn't just here to amuse himself. He was also here for work. He was a social worker and a complaint had come in, one that his employer had handed him late the night before and asked that he look into for him. He didn't want any of the others in the office handling it, he felt it too sensitive. Ben had looked at him and told him that he trusted him to determine if there really was any truth to the matter.

Brandon walked past the booths holding the usual photos for sale, wood craft, hand crafts. He was on a mission. He wanted to find the woman he had been told to find and then enjoy his time. His friends from the Barnabas Foundation had asked him to go with them. He has hesitated and then said he would meet them somewhere at the fair.

Finally stopping near a booth, he frowned. This couldn't be it, he thought. He looked up at the sign: Honey's. It was the name of the company he had been given, but something just didn't seem to add up. Brandon approached, moving around the teenager who seemed to be working the booth, his eyes taking in the educational toys and puzzles. He reached for a wooden doll, feeling the fine workmanship that had gone into it, and then studied all the rest, moving around, a finger coming out now and then to touch a toy or a puzzle. There is no way, he thought, a woman did this. Then he sighed to himself again. No, that's not fair, is it, Lord? You have given them as much creativity and ability and talent to do these as you have a man.

"Can I help you?"

A soft voice with a lilt in it spoke from his left, startling him for a moment, his hand nudging against some of the toys. He reached desperately to keep them from falling over, horror on his face as he imagined the display totally toppling over, breathing a sigh of relief as he did just manage to prevent that very thing from happening.

A gurgle of laughter sounded as he turned. Brandon frowned. This could not be the woman, no, lady, he thought, that we received the complaint about. She was about his age, beautiful, with deep russet coloured hair and wide green eyes with hints of brown and gold and gray in them.

"I'm sorry. I almost destroyed your setup." He grinned, unable to help himself.

"You wouldn't be the first one. The girls and I have a time trying to get them set up sometimes. And there is always one clumsy customer that knocks over a whole display. I must say, you have quick reflexes."

He continued to grin, even as his mind was working through the possibilities. There is no way, he thought, that this lady would be guilty of abuse or neglect. That's what Ben was looking for. Proof that she wasn't.

Brandon pointed to a puzzle. "How do you make those?"

She laughed. "A picture is glued to a board, coats of Varethene applied and then a pattern is traced on top with a China marker. We use a scroll saw to cut the pieces. It sounds easy but it can be complicated. We aim for the younger children, up to about eight years of age, with these."

"I'm impressed. You do this on your own?"

Hagen Daltree. shook her head, turning for a moment to search under the canopy. "My twin sisters help. Holly and Haley. They're sixteen, and this is helping them to cope with our loss."

"I'm sorry. I don't understand." Brandon stepped backwards, to let customers flow by. He was impressed with the professionalism that the teens were showing and how rapidly the products were moving from the tables.

"We lost our parents about a year ago to a car accident. A drunk driver hit them and they didn't survive. Dad died at the scene. Mom died a day later in hospital without regaining consciousness."

"I'm sorry. I lost my parents to illnesses when I was younger than your sisters." Brandon looked around. "Listen. I need to talk with you. Ben asked me to."

"Ben? As in Ben Richards? Why?" A dark look covered her face. "They're at it again, aren't they? Trying to prove I abuse the girls by making them work for me. Or that I neglect them to work on this myself. They just don't get it. I have to do this. I am driven to do this." Tears glistened for a moment in her eyes. "And no, I don't abuse them or neglect. I work on this when they're at school."

Hearing a muffled sound, Brandon looked around, finding one of the teens standing near him, a black look on her face.

"You made her cry. Stop it!"

Brandon's hand went up as he steered Hagen away from the tent and outside. "I'm sorry. I didn't mean to."

"Fix it. And I'm Holly. You'll have to answer to Haley and I if you don't make it better." She glared at him as only a teenager could, then spun and flounced away, eager to find her sister and have her check Brandon out, she thought. He's just perfect for Hagen.

Hagen swiped at her eyes. "I'm sorry. It's just that today is a hard day. We're missing them so much, and then whoever this is keeps calling Ben. He's talked to me, but he was a friend of Dad's and has to step back."

Brandon nodded. "That's why he asked me to step in." He paused in his words, a frown on his face, as he looked around. He could hear the sound of a dirt bike. "I hear a dirt bike. There shouldn't be one here."

Hagen spun. "Not again. Run! He's heading right for us."

Brandon had already reached for her hand, tugging her with him as he ran towards the edge of the fair, thinking it was a blessing that's where she had her tent, heading for the buildings across the street, glad to see there was a break in traffic. He paused for a moment, to stare behind him, seeing the dirt bike waiting, as the rider gunned the throttle, before he began to inch forward. Hagen tugged at his hand this time, pulling him towards a one-story building that stood across from the fairgrounds.

"In here. He can't come in there. At least, I don't think he can."

"He could and likely would." Brandon slammed the door shut. "I need something to block it."

"Here."

Brandon stared in disbelief at the chair Hagen had handed him, before she took it back and jammed it under the door knob.

"That will hold for now. We need to find a way out." Hagen listened. "He's circling the building."

"Trying to spook us, hoping we'll run." Brandon paused, a sound echoing in his ears. "Hagen! We need to leave. Now!"

She spun from where she had been standing near a window, watching their assailant. "We can't. He's still out there."

"Hagen! Now!" Brandon reached for her, even as he felt the floor moving under his feet and ominous creaking sounding in his ears. He wrapped her tight in his arms, as the floor gave way, Hagen's scream echoing with the rending and crashing of the floor. Brandon hit hard, his arms still wrapped around Hagen, trying desperately to protect her and keep her from harm.

The dust swirled around them as debris floated down to settle on them. They didn't hear the screams and then the calls and shouts for help. They didn't hear the sirens as the emergency personnel sped their way. They lay, silent, blood trickling down Brandon's face, Hagen's face tucked against his chest.

Chapter 2

Pausing by the paramedic rig that he had just jumped down from, Brady Coghlan stared at the building, not quite sure what he was seeing. The building looked intact, but word had come that the floor inside had partially collapsed. Someone had reported seeing a couple enter it, seemingly chased by someone on a dirt bike.

This isn't how I planned to end my shift, he thought. I was to meet Brandon here at four, just an hour from now. The call had come in to their dispatch just before three, and Brady and his partner, Patrick had been assigned. Colin, their supervisor, had been apologetic, but with other teams out on the road, he had felt he had to.

Will Peters, chief of police for their town, walked towards him as they rolled their stretcher forward. His hand up to stop them, he hesitated before he spoke.

"Will? What do we have?" Brady's attention was on the building. "Dispatch said something about a couple inside?"

"Yes, they did." Will still hesitated to speak, catching Patrick's eyes, seeing the knowledge that one of Brady's friends were involved.

"Which one, Will?"

———

13

Patrick's words caught at Brady's hearing and he shifted to stare first at Patrick and then back at Will.

"Will?"

"Brady, it's Brandon. I have been told that he was here talking to Hagen Daltree, and then for some reason they ran for the building. Someone passing by heard the sounds of something structural collapsing inside."

Brady paled. "Brandon? I was to meet him here. At four. The rest of our guys and the ladies are here. We had planned to buy our supper and then picnic." He spun back to stare at the activity at the building. "Something doesn't add up."

"No, it doesn't. I wonder why they were in there." Will looked up as a voice spoke beside him. "Alice?"

Alice, one of the patrol officers who had responded, spoke quietly. "The fire chief asked me to come and talk to you. They've been able to see them, but he's not sure how structurally sound the building is. They're assessing that at the moment. He's not sure how long that will take."

"Brandon?"

"The firefighter who was able to lean over the hole said he's not moving. And neither is the lady with him." Alice frowned. "I wonder who she is?"

Will's phone chimed and he stepped away to take the call, his eyes resting on Brady. He sighed as he tucked the phone away. Another one, Lord? Can't these Foundation guys meet their ladies in a normal way?

Alice approached. "The fire chief needs to speak with you." She paused, her eyes on his face, catching the distress he was trying to hide. "Will?"

"Yes, Alice?" Will shook his head, his mind coming back to the present. "Roger needs to speak with me?" At her nod, he pointed to Brady. "Stay with him. I just had word that it's Hagen Daltree who is the lady."

"Hagen? Why?" Alice's face broke from its normal steady look. "It's him again, isn't it?"

"Him? Who? Alice, what are you talking about? Are you friends with Hagen?"

Alice nodded. "More than friends. She's my cousin. Most people don't know that. But, the point is, since their parents were killed and she became guardian to the twins, someone has repeatedly reported her to the social services office for neglect, abuse. Ben can't investigate as he was friends with her father. Unless?" Her voice died away. "Brandon. That's why he was here. I would hazard a guess that Ben asked him to talk to Hagen."

"And being the person he it, he stepped in to help when whatever happened. Do we have any sense of that?"

She nodded once more. "A dirt bike was seen hanging around the end of the grounds."

"And whoever it was chased them. Brandon would have thought they were safe in the house."

—

"Or Hagen would have. She's like that. Thinking of things I would never dream of."

"Like that, is she?"

Alice agreed. "You don't think God brought them together? All the others seem to have to be in danger to find their ladies."

"Not you, though, Alice. You found your life mate, Farr. But you wouldn't have if it hadn't been for Brady and Fynn going through what they did."

"No. I wouldn't have. Not that I would wish that on anyone." Her face litt up as she thought about her boyfriend before she sobered. "Do you want me with Brady or with you?"

"How be you go find the twins? They know you. Stay with them." Will paused. "They're what, sixteen? Who takes care of them if Hagen can't?"

Alice sighed. "That would be me. She didn't know who else to ask, not wanting to put a burden on them, not with what she has been going through. She has had a rough time, Will. She has refused to get us involved, but she has had threats against herself, against her home. Written threats. Emails to her business account. Phone calls. She even said someone has been following her."

"And she never said a word. That doesn't surprise me, but it stops now. When she's able, she will talk to me or to Dallas. Not you. You're involved as family."

"I know." Alice hesitated before she walked away, not sure if she should have said anything to Will. She looked up to see Fynn and Farr heading her way

"Alice? What's going on? We heard a building had collapsed." Fynn hugged her friend.

"It did. I have bad news. Brandon was in it when it went down. He and Hagen."

"Hagen?" Farr whistled in shock. "The girls?"

"I'm heading that way." Alice squinted at the sun. "Will asked me to. Thank goodness it's closing time."

"That it is." Fynn turned to walk with her, Farr standing staring across the street before he headed that way, to stand, his eyes shifting between Brady and the building, knowing how close friends all the men in the building were, all fourteen of them, he thought. All orphans except for Barnabas Carey, the Barnabas Foundation CEO. They were all paid through the Foundation, even though they were employed in the town, leaving their employers free to hire other workers without thinking of the cost.

Lord, their mandate is encouragement. How do we do this now? He paused as he felt someone beside him. Barnabas and Breck stood there.

"Brandon? Did we hear right?" Breck's voice held worry, his face concern.

"You did. I don't know why he's in there, but Alice said Hagen was there."

"Hagen?" Barnabas shot him a look. "She's still not safe."

—

"Safe?" Breck shared a look with him. "Farr, have Alice bring the girls to the building. We'll put them up there for the night. Doc and Anna would take them in."

Farr shook his head, as he watched Brady and Patrick finally moving towards the building, the fire chief and Will heading towards them. They stood before Brady nodded, his hand reaching for the doorframe of the building. He seemed to hesitate before he dropped out of sight, followed closely by Patrick.

Chapter 3

His heart in his mouth for a moment, his professionalism shaken, Brady dropped down from the door to land on the clearest spot he could find. He looked up, seeing how much of the floor had come down. That should not have happened, he thought. It had to have been sabotaged. But why? And who?

Patrick dropped beside him and then reached up for the kits handed down to him.

"Let's assess them, Brady." He moved quickly towards the couple, pausing for a moment, "Brandon seems to have a tight hold on her."

"He does. Let's see what we can do."

Working quickly, the two partners assessed the pair, shaking their heads at one point.

"Backboards and collars, guys." Brady's voice echoed loudly in the building. He reached for the first one and then the second board. "How do we do this?"

"That's a good question." Patrick sat back on his heels before his hands reached for Hagen. "It looks as if they dropped straight now. Brandon took the brunt of it. Let's shift her to the board and then raise her to the guys up top."

Once they had been able to shift Hagen to the board and send her up as Patrick had stated, their attention turned to Brandon.

"Brandon? Can you hear me?" Brady was desperate to know his friend was all right.

Brandon stirred. "Brady? What are you doing here? And just where is here?"

"You've been in a building collapse, my friend. Lay still. Don't even think about moving an eyelash." Brady knew Brandon would try to move.

"I need to get up. Hagen needs me." Brandon lay still at Patrick planted a hand on his chest. "Please? Someone wants to hurt her. He chased us in here. Dirt bike." Brandon's voice faded away for a moment before his groans sounded. "I hurt."

"Where do you hurt?" Patrick shared a look with Brady.

"All over for starters. Can you sit me up?"

"Not a chance, my friend." Brady had been at work as he spoke, the neck collar in place.

"What is that thing? Get it off." Brandon, in his deep need to save Hagen, was starting to become combative, something Brady had not seen with him before. His hands reached for the collar, Patrick's hands there to pull Brandon's away.

"Brandon. Lay still." Brady's hand this time resting on his friend's chest. "We're going to roll you careful to slide the backboard under you. You are not standing up and certainly not climbing out." His hand leaned heavier as Brandon tried to move, to rise, to find Hagen. "Lay still. You're not helping us or yourself. You don't know what you have injured."

"I'm fine. Let me up." Pain shot through him as he moved, his eye closing against it as his consciousness faded.

"He's out again. Good." Patrick reached for the backboard as Brady held Brandon in the position that they had rolled him to. "What's with him and Hagen?"

"I have no idea. I'm not even sure I know who she is."

"She runs Honey's, the educational toy business. I think she's related to Alice."

"Alice?" Brady stood, reaching their kits up to willing hands before he stooped to help lift Brandon. "I've seen her then. Just didn't know who she was."

"That's her. She's had it rough. Brandon will be good for her." Patrick grinned at the look Brady shot him. "He's claimed her, just like the rest of you did."

Brady shook his head, reaching up with the backboard, and when it disappeared, reaching for the hands held down for him.

He was on his knees once more beside his friend, stethoscope in place, even as Patrick started the IV and placed the oxygen mask over Brandon's face.

Will stood, worry briefly crossing his face.

"Brady?"

"He's hurting, Will. I'm not sure where. When we asked him, he stated he hurt all over." Brady looked up, one hand up to shade the setting sun from his eyes. "He mentioned they were chased by a dirt bike."

"A dirt bike?" Will nodded before he walked away, leaving Brady staring after him before he was on his feet, lifting the backboard to the stretcher and then walking quickly towards their rig.

Chapter 4

His eyes moving as he watched the activity around him, Brandon was forced to lie still, the blocks holding his head and the neck collar still in place. He could feel the straps across his body, unable to shift his position other than to move his arms, pain radiating from almost everywhere. His eyes raised as he saw movement near his head.

Doc Andrews, an Emergency Room physician as well as a close friend of the Foundation men, having his own apartment there, stood, watching the monitors on the wall behind Brandon's head before he reached for a wrist. He finally stood, hands on the bed rail, his eyes on his young friend.

"Brandon. What did you do?"

Brandon tried to shrug and then thought better of that idea. "I have no idea. I don't remember. Where was I again?"

"You were at the arts and crafts fair, but somehow ended up in a building that collapsed. Hagen Daltree was with you."

"Hagen Daltree? I don't think I know her." His voice died away. "I was trying to find her, to talk to her. Tell me. Did I?" His whisper held a desperation to it Doc did not understand.

"We suspect so, as she was found wrapped tight in your arms, in the basement of the building as well."

—

23

Doc watched him closely, seeing the agitation in him that was not normal. Brandon was one of the most calm, level-headed men he knew.

"That can't be right. I wouldn't do that. Hold a lady like that." Brandon was becoming more agitated and Doc nodded at the nurse.

"It appears you found her. Now, how you ended up there in the basement, that's what we don't know." He looked around as he heard footsteps. "I'm sending you for a CT scan and some X-rays. I have to, Brandon. We need to determine if you have any broken bones or what's going on. You have feeling in your legs and arms, so I don't suspect any spinal damage."

"I need up, Doc." Brandon's voice had died to a whisper. "I need to find Hagen. She needs me. She's in danger." He slept, the pain medications taking over and sending him unconscious.

Doc shook his head. "Another one." He walked back out to the desk, seating himself, pulling up Brandon's chart to document his findings.

Will watched for a moment before he spoke, Doc shifting to stare at him over his half-glasses before he nodded.

"I'll be right there, Will. We do need to talk."

Will nodded, stepping back to lean against the wall behind him, his eyes watching the activity around him before he noticed Alice standing down the hall from him, her eyes on the room in front of her. He pushed away from the wall, striding towards her, ducking around the personnel mingling in the hallway as they went about their tasks.

"Alice?" Will waited, knowing she had heard him and knowing as well that she would speak.

"Will? Why? Who did this?" She looked up at him, for once not the professional police officer that she was but a hurt and confused family member.

"Alice? What did they say?" He handed her the handkerchief he pulled from his shirt pocket.

"She's hurting, Will. Brandon protected her as much as he could, holding her to him. But she's still hurt." Will's handkerchief twisted in her hands, her upset evident.

Will looked around, spying an empty room, and with a hand on her upper arm, drew Alice into it, almost shoving her down into a chair. He stepped from the room and with a quiet request, was handed a bottle of water. He returned, handing it in to Alice, who twisted it between her hand.

"Talk to me, Alice. What have they said? The younger girls?"

She sighed, looking up, tears sparkling in her eyes. "They're in the waiting room. Anna and Fynn are with them. They were back for a few minutes." She paused, having to swallow hard. "They think she has damage to a hand from a heavy piece of debris falling on it. If she does, she may need surgery. That means she can't work. And she needs to. Not just for the money, but it's her stress release, how she copes with what they've been through. Honey's is named for her mother, but it was a dream that she and her Dad shared, to make the toys and puzzles, to reach out in a way they didn't see others doing. Now what happens?"

Will crouched down in front of her, hearing steps stop at the door. "We'll talk to whoever it is we need to. The girls and you are welcome to go to the Foundation building. In fact, it might be best. Whoever it is may well go after you to get to Hagen. I need you to document everything you can, what she has told you, where she might have put any evidence. I know for a fact that she will have more offers of help than she will know what to do with. It's how our team works, Alice. She and the girls are part of our family. Her father worked with us on numerous cases as an attorney. Our people don't forget that."

"I know, Will. In my mind, I know that. I just don't see how we can go on." Alice blinked rapidly and was on her feet, almost running from the room, searching for Hagen.

Doc stood, Barnabas beside him, watching before Barnabas spoke.

"Cadee and Berneen are working on setting up one of the apartments for them. Burnie and Blair are working to clear out an area in the back of the gym, one of the extra rooms with an outside door, to set up Hagen's woodworking shop." Barnabas rubbed at his temples. Today had not been one of his better days. He had some personal stuff he was trying to deal with, but Brandon came first. "I just got word. There was a fire at Hagen's home. Her workshop is damaged. How bad, we don't know yet."

—

Will had stood as Alice ran, listening to Barnabas speaking. "Her shop? This makes it even worse. How much did she lose?"

Barnabas shrugged. "We're working on that. Brady headed there after his shift ended. Of all the guys, he would be the one best to assess her loss. Farr is with him. They've spent a lot of time over there with Alice and Fynn."

"Good. Find out what you can. I know you well, Barnabas. You've already spoken to your Board. Our association will help with whatever you need. I was telling Alice that officers have come forward to volunteer to help."

Doc nodded. "I heard that. So have staff here. I don't think Hagen or the twins are aware of how well thought of her father was. Her mother as well. She taught just about everyone your age and younger in town at some point, Barnabas."

"She did. I remember having her for a teacher. I think she was one of my favourites." Barnabas pulled out his phone as it chimed, a frown replacing the smile that had crossed his face at his memories. "I need to run, Will. Doc. Let me know what I can do."

They wanted him stride rapidly away, not sure what was going on with him, but raising him up in prayer.

"Brandon? Doc, how is he?"

"I was waiting for some imaging to be done. Barnabas was gone before I could talk with him. He's battered, bruised. No broken bones, but he does have a hairline fracture of his right femur. That will keep him down for a bit.”

“That’s not going to be easy, knowing Brandon. How do we do it?”

“We get Hagen on her feet and to him. They’ve connected, just like the others. She’ll work her magic. I would say she’s not able to go to her own home for now.”

“Not with what I’ve heard. I’ll head over there and then come back. Maybe at that point, one of them will be wake and can talk to me.”

Chapter 5

Hagen shifted in her sleep, one hand coming up to cradle the other, the pain not dulled by the medications. She blinked, her vision blurry for a moment, before she held her eyes open, staring at the cream wall. The line running to the IV bag momentarily distracted her, and she reached for it, fingering it before she let it drop. She shifted once more, turning to her other side, pain filling her eyes with tears before she wiped at them.

Hagen, you do not cry, she told herself. You can't cry. You can't let the twins see you breaking down. You have to stay strong for them. She sighed to herself, knowing the usual pep talk was not working this time. Her head raised from the pillow as she saw a form sleeping in a chair near her.

The person stirred, and she realized it was Brady. Where is Fynn, she wondered?

"Brady?" Her voice was rough for a moment before she cleared her throat.

Brady roused, his eyes popping open as he heard Hagen speak.

"Hagen? You're awake. How are you feeling?"

"I have no idea. I think I was run over by something, only I have no idea what." She shifted again, this time to her back, reaching for the controls to raise the head of her bed.

—

Brady leaned forward, elbows on his knees, to watch her.

"You weren't run over. You ended up in a building where the floor collapsed. They've been around to get your statement, which you did give, but I'm not sure if you even remember that."

She nodded, weary to the bone as her mother would have said. "I do. They said Alice couldn't take it. How long?"

"How long? You mean, how long have you been here? It's about four in the morning, so about twelve hours."

She shifted slightly to her side, so she could study him without turning her head. "You were the one, weren't you?"

He nodded, knowing exactly what she meant. "I was. You weren't on your own."

"I wasn't?" Her eyes slid closed as she pictured the afternoon from the day before. "No, I wasn't. Brandon, was that his name?" At his nod, she sighed. "He tried to save me. I know he fell first. He just wrapped his arms around me. I could hear him praying as we fell. Does he really do that?"

"What? Pray like that? He does. He says his parents taught him that prayer is a day-long conversation with his beloved Father. So, he talks to God about anything and everything. He's got the rest of us started on that. It felt funny at first, none of us thinking of doing that or knowing that was how God wanted us to talk to Him. When he showed us the verse

—

that talks about God being our Abba, our beloved Father, it made it easier." He paused, seeing that she was drinking in his words. "About your hand."

"My hand? How bad?"

"We think a piece of debris fell on it. Some broken bones. Some tendon damage. Doc seems to think you'll make a full recovery." At her cry of protest, his hand went up. "Your work. I know. Barnabas talked to the Board. They can set you up at the Foundation for now." He groaned. "About your shop."

"What about my shop?" She shoved at the bed, forgetting her injured hand until she put weight on it. She sank back, cradling her arm to her chest. "What about my shop?"

"There was a fire there yesterday after we brought you in. Some damage. Will says you can't work there for now."

"I need to, Brady. I have contracts I need to finish. And just how do I do that?"

"With our help, Hagen. The guys have all offered, as have the ladies. Will said he had officers coming forward to volunteer. You'll have so much stock, you'll have to have a sale to get rid of it." He grinned for a moment. "I don't think you know how beloved your parents were."

"I know." Her voice was barely a whisper. "I do know, Brady. That's why I want to do this. It was Dad's dream with me. Mom helped with the planning. I need to follow that dream, to make it a reality. Not just for me. For the twins. They need to see this dream of Dad's come true."

"It will happen. It already has. And the twins are aware of that. Alice took them home a while ago to an apartment in the building."

"I gather we can't stay at our place?" When Brady shook his head, she groaned, her own head dropping back on the pillow. "Then, where? I know Alice would take us in, but it's not fair to her, not when she and Farr are getting married in a couple of weeks."

"Barnabas has had Cadee fix up an apartment for you in the building. He was thinking ahead."

Hagen nodded, her mind already wondering to something else. "Brandon? How is he? He's not dead, is he?"

Brady began to laugh, drawing a frown from her. "No, he's not dead. He took the brunt of it, Hagen. We found you wrapped tight in his arms. Patrick said he claimed you." At her look of outrage, he began to laugh harder. "That's how it is with the Foundation guys. We stake our claim and hold tight." He sobered. "He's battered and bruised and has a hairline fracture in one femur. No concussion, either one of you, which we need to thank God for. Patrick and I could have been picking up you two hurt a lot worse. Or even dead. And that I think was the plan."

Hagen had been watching him, before her eyes slid closed and a single tear rolled down her cheek to drop onto the white pillow case and soak into it. "That's the plan, I think, Brady. Someone wants me dead. And I don't know why."

Chapter 6

Brady had finally made his way home, a yawn stretching across his face. He glanced at the clock and smiled to himself. He would hazard a guess that Hagen was already on her feet, searching for Brandon.

It was true, he would have discovered. Hagen had watched him leave through barely opened eyes, pretending to be asleep, hoping to convince Brady she was, but doubting that she had done that very deed. She slipped from her bed, searching the nearby closet for the bag of clothes Alice had brought her. Appreciation for her cousin's care wafted through her. Alice hadn't been able to retrieve any of Hagen's own clothes so had brought in some of her own. Hagen slipped into them, leaving the gown on the bed, and then shrugged into the zippered sweatshirt Alice had included.

Her sockless feet slipped into loafers, she paced the hallway, searching for Brandon's room. She need to see him for herself, to know that he was alive and not hurt too bad. She didn't doubt Brady's assessment but that was his. She needed to do her own.

Hagen's thoughts drifted to her sisters, and she almost wept in her fear for them. Whoever it was that was stalking her, threatening her, had moved on to threaten them. She needed to keep them safe, but had no idea just how to do that. She sighed again, something she seemed to be doing a lot of lately, she thought, and that was not her. Hagen decided she

—

needed to talk to someone, only she had no idea who. Alice, likely, but she was too close.

She finally found Brandon's room, watching as the nurse exited, making her rounds. The nursed paused for a moment beside Hagen.

"Hagen, can I get you anything?"

Hagen shook her head. "No, I don't think so." She peered past her at the open door. "Can I go in? I need to see Brandon. I need to know he's okay."

The nurse turned to study the room door before turning back to Hagen. "I shouldn't let you, but go ahead. I know what he did for you. If I were you, I'd want to do the very same." She moved past, pausing at the next door to watch Hagen.

Hagen hesitated before she moved forward, her uninjured hand rubbing against the jeans she wore. She paused in the doorway, looking up, asking permission to enter. Finally, her reluctant feet moved her into the room, where she paused once more before moving towards the bed, to stand at the end, her eyes on Brandon's face as his head moved restlessly.

Finally moving to stand near the head of the bed, Hagen's hand reached to grasp the one Brandon was using to pluck at the light blanket covering him. He stilled before his hand shifted from under hers to grasp hers in turn. His grip was tight enough she just could not pull her hand free. Now what, Lord? I can't get away. Is that Your plan? Make me stay? Her eyes slid closed as she prayed for healing for Brandon, not realizing that he had awakened and was watching her, drinking in her beauty, wishing she would open her eyes, eyes that for some reason drew him into their depths.

He was feverish, he knew, not quite making sense of what was going on around him. He shifted in the bed, bringing Hagen's eyes to his, before she gave a small, shy smile.

"Brandon?"

"Hagen, where am I? I thought we were talking at your tent at the fair. This doesn't look like that."

She stared at him, not quite sure how to explain to him what had actually happened to them.

"It's the hospital, Brandon. You were hurt." Her free hand, the one wrapped in a splint and bandages, came up to rest against his chest. "You need to lie still. Please?"

"I can't. I need to find Hagen. She's in danger. Someone is after her. Ben asked me to find her and talk to her." His eyes drifted closed as he licked at his dry lips.

Finally freeing her hand, Hagen reached for the glass of water near him and held it for him to drink from. He finally nodded, his head dropping back on the pillow, his eyes closing for a moment.

Hagen watched him, knowing she should leave, but reluctant to do that, not until she knew he was coherent, and that she had no doubt would take time. She was surprised when he reached for her hand again, his grasp warm on her hand. She felt the strength in his grip, and felt comforted and safe. Now, that doesn't make a whole lot of sense, she thought. I don't know him well enough to say that, but then again, I've heard Brady and Fynn talking about all the men from the Foundation. Guess I trust him without knowing a lot about him.

Brandon's eyes had opened, and his gaze had focused on her. He still wasn't quite sure where he was or even what day it was, but he knew without a shadow of a doubt that he did not want to lose the lady standing there. Only, he had no idea how he would go about keeping her in his life or if she would even want to stay.

He bit at his lip, before moistening them. His mouth felt suddenly dry. Lord, why this lady? Why now? I know she's in danger, but I have no why or who or how to keep her safe.

"Hagen?" Brandon's voice broke through the silence and he winced, thinking that he had spoken too loudly.

"Brandon? You need to be quiet. You have a fever." Hagen tried unsuccessfully to quiet him.

"You're in danger. I need to get up." He tried to raise himself and fell back, helpless for the moment, not seeing the concern and fear that flickered on her face. "I need to keep you safe but I don't know how." His eyes slid closed as the pain intensified. "Marry me, Hagen? Please, marry me. I can keep you safe that way." He slept, not seeing the shock on her face.

A quiet sound drew Hagen's attention to beside her, and she jumped, not having heard Buckley enter. He grinned at her before nodding at Brandon.

—

"How is he?"

"To tell you the truth, I'm not sure. I think that he's dreaming or something." She stared at Buckley for a moment, her eyes narrowing as she did so, knowing he was trying hard to hide a grin and not quite succeeding. "He didn't mean that. I know he didn't. He couldn't have."

Buckley sobered, the panic and hope mingling on her face driving away his mirth. "I think he did, Hagen. I truly think he did. He will remember it and will expect an answer from you." He grinned suddenly, looking like a small boy up to mischief. "I hear tell he claimed you."

Hagen groaned. "Not you too. What is it with you guys?" She flushed. "I'm sorry. I shouldn't have spoken to you like that."

"And why not? Right now, I'm here as Brandon's friend and yours. Not as your minister. So, it's okay to insult me. The other ladies do."

She stared at him, finally remembering to snap her mouth closed. "No, they wouldn't do that."

"On the contrary, they do. Fynn in particular delights in teasing me. But then, I was there when she proposed to Brady."

"She didn't! She wouldn't!" Hagen was shocked, for the moment her troubles driven from her mind.

"But she did. And then he proposed after I left. Ask them." He nodded towards Brandon, seeing his friend's eyes had opened and he was focused on

—

37

Hagen. "He means it, Hagen. In fact, it might be the very best move you could make. You would have the safety and security of the building for you and your sisters, and the companionship of the ladies there. As well, us guys are around. We're a pretty tough lot, when you come down to it. We would be delighted to help solve whatever it is you are facing." A hand up stopped her words. "We know you're facing something. You wouldn't have been chased down by someone on a dirt bike if you hadn't."

"He's right, Hagen. I did mean it."

She spun, her eyes huge, as she became aware that Brandon was awake and had been listening to them.

Chapter 7

Brandon sighed with relief as he settled down in his favourite chair in his living room, glad to set the crutches aside for a moment, his right foot resting on the ottoman. Being as tall as he was, it was no easy task to operate them, he thought. *I'm complaining, Lord. I feel entitled to but I know I shouldn't. But You let us do that, bringing whatever we need or are feeling to You.* He paused, his thoughts drifting for a moment, hearing quiet movement in his kitchen, soft voices talking quietly before he looked up to find Barnabas sitting near him, his head back on the chair, eyes closed, legs stretched out in front of him with his ankles crossed.

"You're wearing out, Barnabas. You need to take a break. What happened with the Langs really threw the Foundation into a turmoil for a while."

Barnabas nodded without raising his head. "It did. They almost succeeded in what they were trying to do. Guenivere and Branigan are fortunate they didn't succeed."

"That they are." Brandon paused, not quite sure what to say.

Barnabas raised his head, staring at his friend, before a grin crossed his face. "I hear you proposed to Hagen."

Brandon shot a glance towards the doorway before he nodded. "I did. I shouldn't have. She deserves to be treated in a special way." He groaned. "I'm not making sense, am I? Must be the pain medications. I don't handle them well."

"Really? I thought you were making perfect sense." Barnabas ducked the small pillow tossed his way, catching it and tossing it back, just as Hagen entered the room, a tray in her hands.

"Barnabas! Really?" She stared between the two men, catching both of them looking sheepish. "Okay. Which one of you started this?"

"He did!" Brandon and Barnabas both spoke at once, fingers pointing at each other, before they broke out into laughter, unable to contain it.

Hagen shook her head. "You're just like two toddlers, caught in mischief." She set the tray down on the coffee table, a little harder than she planned. "I'm sorry. I shouldn't have said that." Horror covered her face as she looked up, ready to turn and run.

Brandon reached for her hand, tugging her over towards him, shifting his foot so she could sit on the ottoman.

"Never apologize for something like that, Hagen. You're correct. We were like toddlers, but you have to understand. We've been through a lot with the guys here. Sometimes, we do goof around, but we would never do it to hurt each other or anyone else. We've been friends for so many years, it feels like we've known each other forever. I left New Brunswick to move here when Barnabas offered me employment."

He stepped at the puzzled look on her face and then sighed. "Barnabas, explain it to her, please."

Hagen shifted to watch Barnabas, finding him intently watching the two of them.

"Barnabas? What does he mean? I don't understand."

"It's this way. The Barnabas Foundation pays the salary for the guys and when they marry, their ladies. That way, their employers can hire someone else and not worry about having to find the finances to do so. It is also a way to encourage others, which as I am sure you know, is the premise behind the Foundation."

"That I knew. I just didn't understand about the salaries. I can understand why you keep it as quiet as you do. You would be taken advantage of, I am sure."

"That is always a possibility." Barnabas reached for a plate and helped himself to the sandwiches she had brought in. "Thank you, Hagen. These look good." He looked around her at Brandon. "I think it's your turn to ask the blessing on the food, Brandon."

"You're right." He reached for Hagen's hand, holding it tightly when she tried to pull it away, a slight shake of his head stopping her. He knew her sisters had entered the room and found seats, and that she was likely ready to run.

Holly and Haley watched their sister closely, knowing that something had happened she hadn't told them. They exchanged glances and then a shrug, before they began to question Brandon about his work.

Hagen's eyes narrowed as she watched the pair, aware of what they were up to. And no, she was not prepared to tell them about the proposal. She thought he hadn't meant it, that it had been his fever, but deep inside, she really did wish he had. She was desperate for someone to share her life and worries. Hagen's life was not turning out how she had planned it, her dreams set aside for now, and perhaps forever. No man would want to marry me, she thought, not and take on the twins.

Brandon had leaned forward to reach for his mug of coffee, pausing as he watched her face.

"I meant it, Hagen. I really and truly did. Buckley will likely come up with a date for us, you know. He did for Fynn and Guenivere."

She turned, almost into his face, seeing his sincerity.

"We need to talk then, I guess, at some point."

"And we will. But for now, you and the girls need to head to your apartment. Just for now. We'll talk tomorrow, Hagen, my darlin'. That's a promise I have every intention on keeping."

Chapter 8

Standing at his office window late that night, Brandon stared out into the darkness, no lights on in the room and just faint light shining from his bedroom. His hand rested on the window frame, his thoughts troubled. He knew that he should have retired but his mind was too active for him to even think about sleeping. His right hand rubbed at his thigh, feeling the pain there, aware that he should be taking the pain medication Doc had insisted that he should do when he had popped in about an hour before.

His eyes drifting up, Brandon's thoughts drifted to Hagen. He smiled as he remembered her outrage at Barnabas over the pillow but then the sudden dampening of her spirit as she tried to back away and apologize for scolding them.

Hagen, he thought, what am I do to with you? Lord, I could use some direction about now. I'm not sure where I'm heading with this beautiful lady or how much danger we'll face. All I know is that I don't want to see her walk away from me. And the twins. Lord, they are such characters but I can see the sorrow in them. How do we reach through that to them?

He finally turned, letting the heavy blue drapes drop back into place, not seeing the man who stood in the shadows near his vehicle, eyes trained on Brandon as he had stood at the window, before he shoved a camera back into his pocket and walked away, heading

———

43

towards the lake and the small boat he had anchored there. He knew where Hagen was, where her sisters were. Now, to find a way to separate the three ladies.

Rising early the next morning, Brandon perched on the side of the bed, his hand resting on his thigh, the pain level higher that morning than he had expected it to be. He heard quiet sounds from the kitchen and nodded. One of the thirteen other men in the building had found their way in and was working on breakfast for them. It was a common plan, breakfast and then prayer when they had an opportunity. He squinted at the clock and sighed. It couldn't be after nine. He never slept that late.

Struggling to shower and then shave, Brandon finally stood, balancing on his crutches, starting down at his feet. He had found a pair of sweatpants, not his usual style of dress, but today he really didn't care. He had struggled to pull on heavy socks, forgoing shoes for the moment. His mind was on Hagen and her problem and how he could best help her.

His crutches thumping along the hardwood floor, Brandon slowly made his way towards the kitchen, pausing for a moment, his head tilting before a smile lit up his face. It wasn't one of the guys, he thought, but Hagen. But who had opened the door for her?

Burnie peeked around the door frame before he appeared in the hall, a tea towel in his hand.

"Brandon, my friend. You are up and on your feet, or foot, rather." He grinned at the face Brandon. "That good, huh?" He peered behind himself towards the kitchen before his voice dropped. "I was heading here this morning. Did you know that Hagen was standing outside your door, just waiting for you to open it? She said she had been there for a while.”

Brandon paused, a frown on his face, before he nodded. “I can see that. She wants to mother, having had to do that with the girls.” He suddenly gave a low laugh. “She told Barnabas and me off last night for tossing a pillow at each other before she apologized.”

“She did? Hmm. I guess you deserved it?” Burnie grinned even wider as he pointed towards the kitchen. “Are you hungry? She had a basket of food for you, did you know that?”

“No, how could I? I haven’t made it to the kitchen because someone is standing in my way and won’t move.” Hagen had appeared in the doorway, a question on her face.

Burnie continued to grin. “Then, I guess I must move and let you by so you can greet your lady. I’m off to my office, Hagen. Come see me when you can. I might be able to help with some of the research you need to do.”

Hagen nodded. “I’ll do that. I need to find some ideas for more toys and puzzles. Thank you, Burnie.” She watched him walk away, not ready to face Brandon yet.

Brandon bit back his grin, knowing she was not going to turn around, not yet. He moved towards her, finally standing right behind her. His crutches went against the wall before he wrapped his arms around her, the toes of the one foot resting on the floor.

Hagen stiffened for a moment before she relaxed, feeling his chin resting on the top of her head. She waited, not sure what to say.

"Hagen? Are you okay this morning?" He felt her hesitation and then nod. "Okay. So. I hear you brought breakfast. Have you eaten?" Once more he felt her head move, this time in the negative. "Then, let's eat. We'll spend some time in prayer, too, if you wish."

She finally moved away, suddenly shy, reaching for the plates she had filled and setting them on the table, one across from the other. Brandon watched her carefully before he reached for her plate, moving it to the spot on the table next to his. She still avoided his eyes, and he bit back another grin, even as he pulled her chair out and seated her, before finding his own seat.

Late that morning, Hagen glanced at her watch, surprised to see how the time had flown. Breck and Brody had appeared a few hours before, simply stating that they were there to take her to her home. The insurance investigator needed to speak with her. Brandon had not given her any choice, simply reaching for his crutches and moving towards the door. She turned as she stood in the centre of her workshop, finding him slumped down on the stool near the workbench, pain evident on his whitened face.

"Brandon? This was too much for you. We should leave."

He looked up, a grin on his face. "No, it's okay. You need to do this. What have you left to do?"

She sighed, her eyes taking in the damage. "Everything here is pretty much ruined. I'll need to start all over, only I don't know how."

His hand reached for hers and stopped her movement away from him. "Barnabas talked to me after you and the girls left. He had spoken to the Foundation Board. They will set you up with everything you need to get back up and running." A finger came up to her lips, to stop her speech, even as he wrapped an arm around her and pulled her to him. Her arm went up instinctively around his neck. "It's what they do, darlin'. This is part of their mandate, how to encourage someone. Bruce, Barnabas' father, was adamant we needed to do this. I think you've been told that there are many volunteers to help you. All we need from you is a detailed list, and I mean detailed, down to the last nail and paintbrush of what you had here and what you would like to have to continue."

"They can't do that." Hagen's voice was barely above a whisper, despair and disbelief in it, but deep in the secret part of her heart, the dream she and her father had shared raised its head once more. If they did that, she could continue and expand. Burnie had sent her text messages, with jokes but also bits and pieces of the research he had taken on. She had protested at that to Brandon, but he had simply shaken his head and say to let Burnie. It's what he did best.

—

Chapter 9

Her arms wrapped tight around herself, the tears she refused to acknowledge trickling slowly down her cheeks, cutting through the devastation and bleakness of her face, Hagen stared around her home. She had finally be allowed in, Will Peters, the police chief, stopping by to assess how she was. She had not expected to find the rooms in shambles, broken ornaments and dishes on the floor, books torn and thrown around. Pictures had been pulled from the wall and the frames and glass on them broken. The food in the fridge and the freezer was tossed around.

Haley and Holly stood beside her, shock on their faces. Their arms reached for their sister and the three stood in a huddled heap, not moving, not wanting to see what the rest of the house was like.

Brandon balanced himself on his crutches, his heart breaking for the three ladies that he had begun to think of as his family. He could hear Will and Barnabas talking just outside the front door. Barnabas had appeared, eager to talk to Hagen to find out what it was she needed to get started. She had just stared at him, unable to answer for her emotions. That was when she had walked away towards the house, the twins appearing on the scene.

He moved forward, letting his crutches rest against the wall, his arms sweeping around the three sisters, his head bowing as he prayed for them. He found feel Hagen relaxing, her body leaning against him, as if in acceptance of what he was offering.

Hagen finally moved away from the security and comfort she found near Brandon, making her way through the house, the devastation and destruction in all the rooms destroying the hope she had begun to feel. She felt someone near her and turned.

Barnabas stood there and behind him stood Alice and Fynn. She simply shook her head, not sure what to say

"Hagen. Tell you what. We'll all pitch in and help you." Barnabas took a look around. "The guys will all be here shortly. The ladies as well. Alice tells me Farr is on his way as is Berneen's brother, Darby. We'll get your home cleaned up for you." He waited for her to respond, a frown on his face as she stood, staring past him before she moved that way. He turned to watch, concerned, before he saw what she was moving towards. A quick movement on his part stopped her in her tracks.

Alice had been watching Barnabas and turned as he reached to stop Hagen. A gasp was drawn from her before her professionalism took over. Her phone was out to call for the crime scene techs before she went on a search for Will.

"Will? I need you to see something. Brandon, we need all of you out of the house for now."

Brandon nodded, his eyes moving towards the twins, a frown on his face as they approached him.

—

"Brandon?   Who would do this?"   Haley struggled to talk, her emotions overwhelming her, Holly's arm around her.

"I don't know but I can guarantee you this. We will find out who and bring them to justice." He looked past her to where Hagen stood, her eyes on him. "We'll let Alice and her friends look around. Then, my friends and the ladies will help you tidy up. Right now, we need to find a place to sit. Your sister has a list to make for Barnabas. Perhaps you could help her with that."

"A list?   Of what?"   Holly's voice had discouragement.

"A list of what she needs to replace from her shop. What her and your wishes are for equipment, material, designs. Mailing stuff. Whatever it takes to get her up and running again."

Holly's face lit up. "We can do that? Honestly?" She spun, her feet taking her rapidly towards Hagen, throwing herself into her sister's arms. "Is that for real, Hagen? We can start making plans to expand, just like you've been dreaming about?"

"That's right, Holly." Barnabas grinned as she peeked around Hagen at him, Haley at her side. "That's absolutely right. The Foundation is setting your sister up again and I have been told by the Board to provide everything that she needs, wants, wishes."

Haley's eyes grew huge. "Hagen! Oh, God has heard us, hasn't He?" She ran towards Barnabas, throwing herself at him to hug him before she danced away, reaching for Holly's hand and pulling her towards the worn-out picnic table that sat midway between the house and the shop.

Hagen had watched them before she turned back to the house, moving closer so that she could watch the activity inside and outside. Brandon moved towards her, an arm around her.

"Why? Why do this? I don't know if the girls saw the message on the living room wall. It was brutal, Brandon. Who threatens to kill teenage girls?" She wept, fatigue and worry uppermost in her emotions.

Buckley spoke from beside her, meeting Brandon's gaze over her head. "God is in control, Hagen. I can't promise that you and heaven help us, the girls, won't go through any more difficulties. But trust me on this. All of us will try our utmost to keep you all safe."

"But that doesn't always work, does it?" Hagen's gaze had drifted towards the large maple tree in the front yard and she broke away from Brandon to approach it. She froze, seeing the enlarged picture of the twins leaving their high school. "That's from yesterday. Whoever it is is watching them." She reached to grasp it, to rip it from the tree, when a hand stopped her. She looked around.

Brendon stood beside her, his hand on her wrist, gently stopping her from the very decd she had contemplated.

"Leave it, Hagen. The police will need to see it. This has become more than just an arson case or your home being invaded. They are stalking your sisters and threatening them."

She gave an abrupt nod. "I know, Brendon. I know I shouldn't touch it. I don't want them to see it."

"But that's the thing, Hagen. We can't shelter them. They need to be aware of this, so that they can take precautions. If we don't and something happens, can you live with yourself?" Brendon watched her face and saw the moment she gave in.

Hagen looked up, trying to cover her feelings, trying to regain control of her emotions, turning as she heard Haley's voice, asking if she had any paper and a pen.

Chapter 10

Late the next morning, Hagen rose from where she had been seated at the kitchen table, searching for her phone, and not finding it. She paused, hand to her cheek, trying to remember where she last had it and sighed. The three of them had been guests once more at Brandon's for supper the night before. That's the last she remembered having it.

Pausing at his door, Hagen finally raised her hand to knock before she turned, ready to walk away, freezing as she saw the man standing behind her. He wasn't one of the building men, that much she knew. She began to back away, before he reached for her, slamming her against the wall, his hands shoving hard against her shoulders. Desperate to escape, Hagen twisted and turned, unable to dislodge his hands, the force just becoming stronger.

His hot breath wafted across her face, the smell of alcohol and tobacco smoke causing her stomach to churn. He didn't say a word, just stared down at her before he gave a hard shove and then sauntered away, heading for the back stairs.

Hagen dropped to the floor, her head buried against her knees, shaking as she had never shaken in her life. She was terrified. Just who had that been? And why? Who was it that was after her, trying to destroy her dream, threatening her sisters?

—

She didn't look up as she heard footsteps, not seeing Brody stopping on the other side of Brandon's doorway before he knocked and then opened it, calling for Brandon. Brandon appeared, puzzled that Brody had not entered, before his eyes followed Brody's pointing finger.

He was beside Hagen, his crutches cast aside as he dropped to the floor, his arms cradling her, not understanding why she was fighting him, that was, until she heard his voice and then turned to him.

"Who was that man?" Her question stopped both men before they could ask anything, as they stared at her and then at one another.

"What man?" Brody stood, ready to search for whoever it was.

"That man! Where did he go? He shoved me against the wall. Hard. And wouldn't let me go. He threatened me. No, he didn't say anything, just his look and the force he held me with." She looked up at Brandon. "Please make him stop."

Brody turned and was gone on the run, flying down the stairs and then sliding to a halt at the security desk. The guard shook his head, before his fingers were moving quickly on the keyboard, pulling up the feed from the last little while. Brody stared in disbelief as they watched the man appear and then disappear through the back door.

"I thought we solved the problem of people accessing that." Brody was frustrated. It was not the first time someone had entered there, intent on nefarious purposes.

"We did." The guard was moving, heading for the door, Brody on his heels, his phone out to call Barnabas and then the police

Brandon finally managed to stand, taking the crutches Hagen handed him, his hand resting on her cheek.

"Are you hurt?"

Hagen shook her head. "I don't think so. Just shaken." Her anger was beginning to boil over once more, as her mother would have said. "I thought I was safe here."

"And you should be. Let security figure it out. Right now, in there." He pointed at his door. "I have your phone and was just about to head up with it when Brody knocked."

"That's why I'm here. I thought I had left it here." Hagen moved around the kitchen, finally reaching for the kettle, filling it and then lifting the coffee carafe before she dumped it out and made fresh. She could not settle to sit, her mind racing as to what the man had wanted.

Brandon watched her, seeing the conflicting emotions on her face, before he moved to stand in front of her, stopping her with a hug. She stiffened for a moment, before her arms hugged him back.

"What am I do to with you, darlin' Hagen?" Brandon's voice was soft in her ear. "Marry me? Let me protect you and the girls."

Hagen froze, her head on his chest, hearing his heartbeat in her ear. Lord? What do I do? Do I take his offer or refuse it? Is it fair to him, if I do? She waited, waited for God's leading, waited for the peace she should feel.

She finally nodded, her voice muffled somewhat as she spoke. "It's not fair to you, Brandon. What if we do marry and you find someone else?"

Brandon simply shook his head, reaching to tuck a russet curl behind her ear, one that had escaped her braid. "That won't happen, Hagen. I can promise you that. God has led so far. I have peace with asking you that. What about you?"

Hagen moved back enough to stare up at him, his arms loosening around her. "I do, I guess." She groaned. "That's not fair. God has not put a roadblock in place, I know that." She shifted from foot to foot, suddenly nervous, not quite sure what decision to make.

Brandon nodded, before his head bowed, his prayer raising for the lady he had grown to love with all his heart in such a short time, asking for wisdom in their decision, and that if it wasn't in God's will, that they would know.

Hagen turned when he finished, reaching for their mugs, hesitant as to where to sit.

"Hagen? How be we sit out on the balcony? I've been inside all day and could use some fresh air." Brandon grinned at her, and she froze, seeing in a moment, in the man standing in front of her the man who had haunted her dreams for years.

"Sure. Do you want anything to eat with your coffee?" Hagen was desperate to busy her hands, not sure if she should be even asking that.

"Not unless you do. I had a sandwich a while ago."

"No, I'm fine." She headed past him for the living room before his voice stopped her

"There's a balcony off the office. That's my favourite spot. I would like to share it with you."

She turned. "You have an office here?"

"A home office. I also have one on the main floor. Barnabas set us all up with one." He pointed down the hall. "Take a look in the rooms as we go by. Now, the girls? Do they share a bedroom or have their own?"

She blushed for a moment, the rosy colour on her cheeks fascinating Brandon who thought she looked even more beautiful. "They have their own but they could share."

"Not a problem. We can ask them."

Hagen nodded, even as she paused in each doorway, taking in the colour scheme, which was so much like hers. Creamy yellow walls in all the rooms gave a consistency that pleased the artist in her, contrasting with the dark wooden floors. Colourful drapes in all the room, each a different colour, set a tone that she liked. She paused in his office, staring around.

"This is nice, Brandon. I like it."

"Good. There's room in here to set up another desk for you. The girls will have a desk in each of their rooms." He waited for her to exit the office before he sank down in one of the brown wicker chairs, reaching to pull the ottoman over to raise his leg.

Hagen had been watching him closely. "Your leg?"

"It hurts but not like it did. Doc's been watching me."

"That's good. I just hate that you were hurt because of me."

"I'm not." Brandon raised his eyes to find her staring at him in shock. "Let me repeat myself, Hagen. I am glad I was there. Even getting hurt? I can live with that. What I can't live with would have been you being hurt or killed."

She nodded. "What happens with your investigation of me?"

"I talked to Ben last night. He's not going any further with it. In fact, he has go to the police services and put in a report of harassment on your behalf."

"He has? He didn't have to,"

"No, he did. It was a false report, many of which he has received. It needs to be documented with the authorities."

Chapter 11

Staring at their sister before looking past her at Brandon, who stood, his hands on her shoulders, Holly and Haley were dumbfounded. They had talked about that very possibility, that Brandon would sweep in and save them, but never expected it to happen.

"You're engaged? Wow!" Holly finally reached to hug her sister, finding Brandon waiting to hug her as well.

Haley stood, not sure of what to say or do, before she stood in front of Hagen, searching her face.

"It's not because of us, is it, Hagen? I know you've had threats against us." She tried to control her emotions. "I didn't tell you. Someone has been following us. I don't know if Holly saw him."

Holly turned, Brandon's arm still around her shoulder. "No, I didn't. You didn't tell me."

"I wasn't sure at first. I saw him again today when we left school. He was walking towards us until he saw Breck waiting for us and then he left."

Brandon grew grim. "We'll need you to talk to the police. It's an active investigation."

Hagen nodded even as she reached for Haley. "I wonder if it's the same man."

"What man? Hagen, what aren't you telling us?"

"There was a man in the building today, who threatened me. Brody was looking into it." Hagen sighed. "This is not working."

Brandon's arm was around her as she spoke. "It will work, darlin'. It will work." He suddenly grinned, the twins staring at him, both with narrowed eyes. "This calls for a celebration. I would like to take all my ladies out for dinner."

"You would?" Holly's face lit up. "Oh, can we, Hagen?"

Her face tilted up to Brandon, she communicated with him in silence before she nodded. "I think we can do it. Is it safe enough, Brandon?"

"It should be. Brody and Burnie are heading in to town for a meal. We can all go together. I think they were heading for that little Italian place."

"Oh. Dress up?" This from Haley.

Brandon had not intended that, but at the excitement and eagerness on the twins' faces, he could not say no. "Sure. Why not?"

"Okay. Hagen, come on. You need to change. Dress up is not those jeans and T-shirt." The girls dragged her away, protesting, even as Brandon grinned in sympathy with her.

"They seem excited." Barnabas spoke from beside him. He had been watching the interaction between Brandon and the girls, a grin on his face at how they were reacting to him.

"They are." Brandon stared towards the spot they had disappeared in. "Just so you know, Hagen and

I will be getting married, as soon as we can. Today really rattled her.”

“I know. Are you sure, Brandon? I know you will have prayed about this.”

“I’m sure. So is she.” Brandon looked down at the floor, a bleak look on his face for a moment. “It’s not how I imagined it would happen.”

“None of the guys have, but they met the ones God meant for them.” Barnabas nodded into the distance where Hagen had disappeared. “She’s your lady, Brandon. We all can see it.”

“She is, Barnabas. She is. I just don’t know how to tell her that.” Brandon turned, his crutches thumping on the floor, before he walked away from Barnabas, his apartment door shutting quietly behind him.

A couple of hours later, Brandon shifted in his seat at the table in the restaurant, uncomfortable for a moment, the feeling of being watched niggling at him. He couldn’t see anyone that was overtly keeping an eye on their table, but the twins’ excitement and chatter had drawn eyes and smiles their way throughout the meal. Hagen had tried to tamp down their chatter, but finally gave up, a shrug showing it was normal when they were excited.

Brandon reached for her hand, his clasp warm, before he leaned over.

“I take it they’re not upset at our news.”

Hagen shook her head, a smile on her face, before she spoke. “If they had been, you would have known. They can be vocal that way. They have always said what they feel." She shivered, her eyes searching the room or what she could see. "Someone's in here, Brandon. I can feel them watching us."

"I know. I have had the same feeling." He looked up as Brody stopped by their table, a grin on his face as the twins greeted him.

"Ready to head home, ladies? We can offer you a ride if you like. Brandon seems to have settled in here for the night."

Brandon simply shook his head. "No, we're good to go. Ladies, are you finished or do we need to wait longer for you?"

Haley stared at him, her eyes narrowing as she caught the grin he was trying to hide. "No, I think we're finished. Brody?"

"I would say you were. We'll be at the door." He shared a look with Brandon, who simply nodded.

Hagen had been watching the two and knew from the looks shared between then that her feeling had been accurate. They were being watched.

Brandon shifted on his truck seat, turning to talk with the twins in the back seat but obstensively to watch out the back window. Hagen kept glancing at him and he finally shook his head.

"Someone's back there?" Hagen kept her voice low

"I think so. With Brody behind us, they won't try anything. Not like what happened with Brady and Fynn."

—

"It was along here, wasn't it?" Hagen paled, remembering how Fynn had told her about the accident they had had.

"It was." Brandon breathed a sigh of relief as she turned in to the parking lot of the building. "We're home. Let's meet tomorrow, Hagen. We need to talk, but we also need to see if we can come up with some names."

She nodded. "I need to start working. My orders are backing up." She parked the truck, turning off the ignition and then handing him the keys. "Thank you, Brandon, for our meal. And thank you for being who you are."

Chapter 12

The next morning, Hagen stared around her new shop, shock on her face, not quite sure what to say. She had not expected to see it up and running, not when she had just given Barnabas her list, what two days ago, she thought? This is amazing. Lord, it has to be You. That's the only explanation. She wandered around, touching the new equipment, the stain and paint cans set up at a nice large table that was covered with a laminate, easy to clean off, she thought. She looked at the wall beside it, seeing brushes in all shapes and sizes that would work for her crafts. She moved on to where the display shelves stood, a hand reaching out to touch them, before she once more walked further into the shop, seeing the stacks of wood on shelving, the papers and plastic laminates she would need.

Hagen stopped in front of another huge counter, this time, awe on her face. A shipping table, she thought. No more moving things around to pack her wares. No more packing them in the kitchen. A desk stood nearby, with a large printer and laminating machine beside it. Shelving behind the table held myriads of packing material and labels.

She stood, tears on her cheek. Dad, it's come true. Our dream has come true. We have a professional shop to work from. I just wish you were here. I need you to see this. Her tears continued unabated even as she felt gentle hands turning her into a body and arms hugging her tight. Brandon had found her. His chin

---

rested on the russet head, even has his hand traced her braid.

"Hagen? What's the matter, darlin'? Did we miss anything? Haley and Holly gave a quite a list, but if there is something we need to add, we can." Brandon's voice whispered in her ear.

Hagen shook her head, unwilling to move away from him. "No, I don't think you did. It has everything I have dreamed about, in the way I wanted to set it up. The girls must have given you my plans."

"Fynn and Alice helped. In fact, all the guys and the ladies met with your sisters. They are quite opinionated, did you know that?" He gave a grin she couldn't see. "Haley and Holly laid it all out. What you wanted. What your father had wanted. What your mother had suggested. We just took it all and combined it. This is what came up. I just need to know. Is it what you want? What do you need changed?" Brandon shared a look with Breck who stood in the doorway, knowing that Hagen had headed that way.

Hagen raised her head to look up at him, wondering how she had managed to find a boyfriend so tall. That was not what she had planned.

"It's fine, Brandon. It's fine. I just didn't expect it, that's all." She turned, his arms loosening enough to let her. "It's Dad's dream. I just wish he was here. I need him to see this, and he's not."

Breck walked towards her. "Then, let's see what we can do to get you doing more. Blair wants to work on a website for you." He held up a hand. "I know,

—

you have one. It's good, but Blair does that for a living for some people. He just wants to help. If you say no, that's fine."

Hagen stared at him. "I don't know what to say, honestly." She reached into a pocket of her jeans and pulled out a paper. "Maybe one of you can figure this out. I found it taped to the door this morning. Someone knows where I am and where my shop is. How do I keep all of you safe if that's the case?"

Breck's face hardened as he took the paper and read it. "I'll pass this one for you, Hagen. Dallas has been assigned to your case. He'll want to talk with you." He looked around. "Now, where do we begin?" He broke into a sudden grin. "I've always wanted to try my hand at woodworking."

She stared at him, before shaking her head. "Really? Just set that aside." She pointed at the paper. "I don't know that I can. Not that easily."

Breck studied her, realizing he had misread her and underestimated her feeling. "Hagen, I apologize. I did not mean to discredit your feelings or the danger you are in. Whoever this is means business. We have seen that. We need to sit down and go back over everyone you know, that may have a grudge against you or your family."

Hagen nodded, before moving away, heading for the filing cabinet and pulling open a drawer. She slapped a folder down on the table. "Here. This is what I have. Everyone and every business I can think of. There may be more and that we can figure out." She turned back to the cabinet, her back stiff, before she pulled out patterns and then moved away from the men, to reach for wood and her tracing pencils.

Breck and Brandon exchanged a glance before Brandon spoke in a low voice.

"She's hurting, Breck. Not just from that. With our plans she is missing her Mom. She hasn't told me that. Haley did."

"I am sure she is. The other ladies want to meet with her, to help with plans, but they're unsure if she wants them to. With Alice and Farr getting married this weekend and with what she's been facing on her own, her emotions are likely a mess."

Chapter 13

Finally looking up, her right hand worried the bandages and splints on her left hand, Hagen searched the room, seeing activity in just about every area. She had turned from her table hours earlier when Brandon had wrapped an arm around her and told her she had company. What did she want them to do, he asked?

Hagen had been surprised to see all the men there as well as the ladies. Doc and Anna had stood and watched as Buckley had prayed for her and for her work. She had not been able to say a word, her surprise that complete. Holly and Haley she could see near the mailing table, packing up what they had been able to salvage and repair, with Darby, she thought his name, Berneen's brother. She stretched as she rose, wandering the room, greeting each one, answering their questions, thanking them with tears in her eyes that she could barely contain. They had more than made up for the time she had lost and what had been lost in the fire.

Reaching the outside door, Hagen shoved it open, standing for a moment in the late day sunlight, feeling the fall chill coming. Early fall or autumn or whatever you wanted to call that season before winter, she thought, is one of my favourite times of the years. It gives me incentive to keep going, to be outside, to enjoy the wonderful works of God, to find ideas for her work. She was in the planning stages of a woodland set, trying to work through the intricacies of it.

—

Brandon stood for a moment, the door leaning against his arm, before he hobbled forward to where Hagen stood.

"You okay?" His voice was quiet, not sure how she had felt about them all descending on her. He had heard the comments over the hours, how they liked her work, that it was really great for the children she was trying to read. Burnie, the author of the group, had turned at one point, a question on his lips, that died as he studied Hagen, before he shook his head. He wanted to use her handcrafts in a book idea that had come to him as he worked. He could talk to her later, he decided.

"I am, my love. That I am." Brandon's eyes shot to her at her words of endearment, not sure if she meant them or not. "I didn't expect them all to show up, though. They've caught me up to where I wanted to be weeks ago and couldn't get there." She looked up, a pensive look on her face. "How do I thank them?"

He reached to wrap her in his arms, content to stand near the garden entrance, not wanting to move away. "You did, just by how you reacted now. They don't want thanks, darlin'. They live to serve. I can guarantee you that they will be around when they can to help. You'll never be behind again."

She leaned her head back against him. "Then, that's that." She paused. "Brandon, are you sure?"

"Sure? About what? About us?" He felt her nod. "I am, darlin' Hagen. That I am. You are my heart, the one God planned from before time to be my helpmeet. I love you, Hagen. Never doubt that. I never believed in love at first sight, not until I met you." His head tilted as he looked at her face. "And you? You're sure?"

She hesitated for a fraction of an instant, causing him to despair, before she spoke. "I am, I think." She groaned. "That's not how I meant it. I am sure. I just need to be sure the girls are okay with it."

"And I can assure you that they are. Both came to me this afternoon, on their own, and thanked me for choosing you."

"They did? Wow! I guess that's that then." She looked away from him. "Brandon! Someone's here."

"There is. Run, Hagen. Head for your shop. I'm behind you."

Hagen began to run, hearing the thump of Brandon's crutches behind her until she heard a shout from him and slid to a stop, spinning to see him on the ground, not moving. Her eyes raised to the man standing over him and her heart sank. He was back. She retreated, not quick enough before arms wrapped around her from behind. She struggled to escape, unable to free herself and felt herself picked up and carried back towards where Brandon lay.

Set on her feet, an iron grip on her wrist that she could not escape, Hagen stared at the man, refusing to speak.

"So, you're back up and running? You don't listen very well. It would be a shame for something to happen to that building." The man standing over Brandon walked around him, to stand in front of her, close enough that she could once more smell the alcohol, tobacco and sweat coming from him. "Not talking? That's okay. You don't need to talk." He turned for a moment to stare down at Brandon and then turned back to stare past her at the building.

"Come on, man. Do what you have to and let's get out of here." The man holding her was getting edgy and nervous. He figured it would only be a matter of time before someone came out and saw them.

"Hold your horses. I'm getting there." The first man, his hair, face and clothing dirty and unkempt, stared at Hagen before a fist headed her way, driven into her ribs.

Hagen cried with the pain, feeling her ribs give way. Her wrist was released and she fell to her knees, her arms wrapping around herself, tears of fright and pain on her cheeks. Her last coherent sight was seeing his foot raised and headed for her. She didn't feel the heavy steel-toed boot driven into her before she collapsed to the ground, to lie motions less just feet from Brandon.

The men stood over the couple before they shrugged. The older man pulled out a dirty once-white envelope from a pocket, studied it, and then dropped it onto Hagen's body before they moved away rapidly, suddenly aware that others would be coming out of her shop and they needed to disappear before they were caught.

Chapter 14

Laughing at something Brennen had said, Bradon and Brody headed out the door, the three men standing for a moment, sensing something off before they shrugged. Brennen was uncomfortable about walking away, his eyes searching through the dusk, before, with a cry for help, he was running away from the other two men. Bradon took off after him, Brody heading back in for Brady who was still around, knowing that if they needed help, their paramedic friend was the one to bring. His sudden reappearance startled the men and they rose, heading for the door, admonishing the ladies to stay inside. Haley and Holly reached for each other, just then realizing that Hagen wasn't in the shop. Fynn and Ennis moved towards them, asking questions to divert their attention.

Brennen dropped to his knees beside Brandon, a hand reaching for a pulse, his head dropping for a moment as he realized that Brandon was alive. It raised as he heard Bradon's cry of alarm, to find him on his knees beside Hagen, a hand reaching to push back her hair and then both hands in motion, trying to find out what was wrong.

Brady's steps slowed before he was on his own knees, assessing Brandon.

"It looks as if he was hit from behind. I can feel a knot on the back of his head. His leg?" Brady looked up at the question from Brendon. "I'm not sure. If he fell wrong, he could have injured it. We need the teams here."

Brady was on his feet, moving rapidly the few feet to where Hagen lay. He rolled her carefully to her back, hearing the moans that came from her as her arms wrapped around her abdomen. He didn't like the trickle of blood that came from her mouth.

"Brady?" Barnabas crouched down beside him, the other men standing with their back to the group, on guard, watching for anyone who was not to be there.

"She's hurt somewhere in the abdomen. The ribs, too, from what I am feeling." Brady sat back on his feet. "Who and how? I would hazard a guess that she's got fractured ribs and from how she's trying to hold her abdomen? She's hurt there." He turned as he heard the sirens approaching. "Good. We'll get them in and get them assessed." He looked up at Barnabas. "Who tells the twins?"

Barnabas sighed. "That would be me, I guess. Hagen talked to me the other day, asked that if anything happened to her, before she and Brandon married, would I take on the care of the twins? They have no one else. We were in to the lawyers that day to sign the paperwork. Brandon as well."

"Good." He stood, giving his assessment to the paramedics who had approached before he stepped away, to stand beside Breck and Barnabas. "I'll ride with Hagen. Who's with Brandon?"

"Brendon is. He's not leaving his side, he said." Breck turned for a moment, seeing Dallas approaching.

"Dallas is here. Head off, Brady. He'll catch up with you in town."

Dallas stood beside the two men, watching as the stretchers holding the couple were wheeled away, many hands ready to help as the men from the building walked beside them. He watched as well as Barnabas stood, arms around the twins, their hands clinging to each other before he moved them away towards his vehicle, Fynn and Ennis with them.

"What happened?" Dallas turned to Breck.

"We don't know. They walked out and then a while later some of the others came out and found them. Whoever it is, I must say, is really bold. This is the second time they've come after Hagen on our land."

"It is. How do we stop them? With the forest surrounding you and then the lake not too far away, you can't fence it."

"No, we can't. We've never had a need to, not until lately." Breck spun. "Someone is still out there, watching us. I can feel him."

"I know." Dallas looked around, motioning to some officers, sending them off on a search. "We'll not likely catch them. I just pray we're not too late."

Breck nodded. "Almost losing Bradon and Fynn was bad enough. I don't want to see it happen to anyone else." He watched as Dallas headed away towards the shop, where Buckley stood waiting.

Watching carefully, Brady stood in a corner of the examination room, out of the way, as Hagen was assessed. He sighed. It was what he thought. A punctured lung. Abdominal injuries. There was talk that she would need to head for surgery. He left, intent on finding Barnabas, stopping as he saw Doc heading his way.

"Doc? I didn't know you were working tonight."

"I wasn't supposed to but Jeff called me, asking me to cover for him. His wife took sick and they had to head for Toronto to see her specialist there first thing in the morning."

"I see." Brady turned to walk back down the hallway with him. "I don't like what I'm seeing with Hagen."

"Me, either. I'm sending her for imaging. Just what happened?" Doc was angry, angry that friends had been ambushed once more on their home property.

"We don't know. Some of the guys had left her shop and found them." Brady paused outside another examination room. "How's Brandon? What damage was done to him?"

"So far, it seems as if he was just knocked unconscious. The leg is healing from what we can see on X-Ray. In fact, I think he can go to a cane when he leaves."

"That's good news. Now, about Hagen? What do we tell the twins?"

Doc shook his head. "I'll be out in a few minutes. Tell them I'll come talk to them." Doc peered over his half-glasses at Brady. "Who are they with?"

"Fynn. Ennis. And I think the other ladies. Someone had gone for Anna. I talked to Farr. Alice had to be out of town today to testify in another case. He's trying to reach her."

"Good. Go on, Brady. Find the twins. Stay with them for now." Doc shoved open the door and disappeared inside, the door swinging silently shut behind him.

Chapter 15

Brandon stirred, a hand reaching for the back of his head, as his eyes flickered open and closed. He finally managed to crack them open partway, before blinking to clear his vision. A hospital room. Now what did I go and do? I don't remember. I don't remember things for a few weeks now. I have no idea what day it is. Hearing a sound beside him, he turned, frowning at the two young ladies who stood, worry on their faces.

"Brandon? You're awake? Are you okay?" The one who was slightly taller, her hair a beautiful red gold and having dark brown eyes, spoke.

"Yeah. I think so. Where am I?"

"You're in the hospital." This from the other girl, who had the same red gold hair but hazel eyes. "You scared us."

"I'm sorry. I didn't mean to. When can I leave?" He raised himself up, only to fall back down again.

"You can't leave yet, Brandon." Breck spoke from the other side of the bed. "Doc says you're staying overnight." He looked over at the twins. "Haley and Holly stayed just to see you were okay. Brady's heading home with them."

Brandon gave a small nod, a hand raising in a wave as the twins turned to walk away, their heads keeping turning to watch him

---

As the door closed, Brandon's head went back and his eyes closed for a moment. "Who were they?"

Breck stared at him. "What do you mean, who are they? They're Haley and Holly, Hagen's sisters."

"Hagen? Who's she?"

"Hagen? What do you mean? Who's she?" Breck stared at him.

"What I said. Who is she?" Brandon's eyes finally stayed open and he stared up at Breck.

"Hagen? Brandon! She's your lady. You're engaged to her. Those two are her sisters she's guardian to. What do you mean?"

Brandon sighed. "I don't remember her. Not at all. What day is it?" When Breck told him, Brandon stared at him. "That can't be right. Not at all. Didn't Branigan and Guenivere just get married?"

"Like about three months ago. Brandon? Are you saying you don't remember three months?"

Brandon sighed, his eyes closing. "I guess I am. What happened?"

"You and Hagen were attacked on our property. You two had left her shop. Some of the guys found you when they followed about thirty minutes or more after that." Breck ran his hands through his hair. "You really don't remember."

Brandon shook his head and then groaned. "You just had to have me do that. I don't know who she is. How did we meet?"

"You were at her booth at the arts and crafts sale for some reason. You two were talking and then were chased by someone on a dirt bike. You ducked into that old Farmer house and the floor collapsed, which it shouldn't have. The same day, she had a fire in her workshop at her home. Barnabas had her move into the building. You're in love with her, Brandon. How can you not remember?"

Brandon stared at the door, reaching for the bedside and raising himself up, waiting until his head cleared before he swung his feet over the side, balancing for a moment, a hand going to his thigh. "What did I did?"

"You had a hairline fracture there from the building collapse. Brandon? What are you doing?" Breck watched as Brandon hobbled to the closet, retrieved his clothes and then headed into the bathroom, before he reappeared, fully dressed, a hand resting on the wall.

"I want to see her. Now. If what you say is true, then take me to her."

Breck simply shook his head, reaching for the wheel chair. "You ride in this, or I won't take you."

Brandon nodded, at the end of his strength for the moment, before he pointed to the door. "Now, Breck. I want to see her for myself, to see if I do remember."

Barnabas and Brennen stood watching, seeing Breck's shrug at them, before they followed him down the hallway, stopping outside a room door. Breck's hand reached to push it open and then paused.

—

"Brandon, before you go in, pray, which I know you have been doing. If you don't remember her and tell her that, it will destroy her. She and the twins lost their parents a year ago to a drunk driver." His voice died away before he spoke again. "Now, I wonder." He spun to face Barnabas. "Has Dallas looked into that?"

"I'm sure he has. I'll mention it to him." Barnabas' eyes raised to stare down the hall, seeing both Will and Dallas walking towards them. "In with you two. I'll stall them."

Will stood, his eyes on the door, before he turned to Barnabas. "He's up and about?"

"He is, but somehow, I don't think it's good. Breck looked stressed when he wheeled him down this way."

Dallas shook his head. "Then I guess I'll need to talk to him." He looked around Will as Breck reappeared. "Breck?"

"We have a problem, guys. Brandon does not remember Hagen. Nor the twins. He thinks we're still living three months ago."

Chapter 16

Pausing just near the bed, Brandon's eyes slid closed as he prayed. Lord, I don't remember this lady, even though Breck says I do and that we're engaged. I just don't know, Lord. How do I get to remember? Please, Lord, I don't want to hurt her.

Wheeling himself up the bed, Brandon's eyes first took in the monitors around Hagen, then the lines with the IV and plasma running to her arms. He shook his head. What had happened to her? He wished he could remember her.

His gaze dropped to her face, seeing the whiteness, no, gray look, he thought. What happened to her? He reached for her hand, the one with the splints and bandages, now replaced with clean ones. Brandon shook his head as he once more raised his face to watch her, seeing her eyes flickering open as she roused.

Hagen roused, not sure where she was, only knowing that she hurt, and hurt badly. She sighed to herself as she remembered the men, knowing one had already been stalking her. She needed to talk to Alice, no, not Alice. Was it Dallas who she needed to find? She felt her hand being held and nestled her fingers tighter to the man's hand, that she was sure of. It had to be Brandon.

Looking around, she finally spied him, his eyes glued to her, a puzzled look on his face. Licking at her lips, she was finally able to speak.

"Brandon? You're okay? I didn't know what they had done to you." She frowned as he didn't speak. "Brandon?"

He shook his head. "I'm okay. Just a bad headache. And whatever it was I did to my leg. And you?"

Hagen continued to frown, sensing something different. "Brandon?" She groaned as the pain hit and then she was away, unable to finish her conversation.

Brandon waited before he finally pushed away and wheeled to the door, struggling to open it and maneuver through. Brennen was heading his way and nodded at the door.

"How is she?" Brennen waited, puzzled at the look on Brandon's face and the length of time he took to answer.

"I'm sorry, Brennen. I just don't know." He wheeled past his friend, heading for the waiting room. He needed to go home, to be somewhere he knew where he was and to sort through his thoughts.

Brennen stared after him, not quite sure what to think. He looked back at Hagen's door before he walked after Brandon, hearing his request for someone to drive him home. Breck rose, shaking his head, before he pushed Brandon away, leaving the few who had gathered there to stand, staring after them, dumbfounded at Brandon's words.

—

Brennen stared behind him before he spoke. "What's that all about? Why is he leaving when Hagen's still here?" At the silence that greeted his words, he turned.

"He doesn't remember her, Brennen." Brady spoke, Fynn's arm around him. "He doesn't remember her, the twins, or even that he asked her to marry him. He thinks we still living just after Branigan and Guenivere were married."

Brennen stared at him before he shook his head, a groan coming from him. "Now, what? How do we get him to remember?"

"I talked to Doc about that possibility." Barnabas spoke up. "We talked about a number of issues he could face. It takes time, Doc said, or else it will take Hagen being in difficulty again for him to remember. And then again, he might never remember."

"And just how do we tell the twins? Haley and Holly adore him already. To have him walk away would be like losing their parents all over again." Brennen turned and stalked away, anger rising in him. Anger at Brandon. Anger at the world. Anger at the men who had done this. Anger at whoever it was behind them. He was determined to find them and headed for his truck and then the Foundation building, walking rapidly through it to the conference room, unlocking the door, flicking on lights in an angry manner before he slumped into the chair he preferred.

Lord, forgive me. I don't have the right to be angry. It's not my life. But it's a friend and his lady.

—

Help me to help them. Let me find some clue, some word, some person, some business that will unlock this mystery. I don't want to see them hurt any worse. He prayed for healing for Brandon. For Hagen, he hesitated, knowing that her condition was serious. A punctured lung, he thought, and internal bleeding. He shuddered at the words Doc had spoken to them all, that whoever had kicked Hagen had done so with work boots and with force. She was fortunate, he said, that she survived.

Chapter 17

Two days later, staring in disbelief at Brennen, Hagen shook her head, slumping back on the couch in her living room. She had been stunned with his response to her question of where was Brandon and was he all right.

"That's not true, Brennen. It can't be true." The hurt she felt showed on her face, her mind unable to comprehend that the man she loved and who had said he loved her, didn't remember her any more, in fact, had not been around her.

"I'm sorry, Hagen." Brennen sat on the coffee table, facing her. "Doc said it was the blow he took, that caused him to forget."

"No, it can't be true. Haley and Holly are looking for him. Doesn't he realize how much he means to them, to me?" Hagen's eyes slid closed. "That's why he was like he was."

"When?"

"In the hospital. He just didn't seem himself, not the man I know." She looked up, shadows on her face and in her eyes. "What do we do? How do we get him to remember?"

Brennen shrugged, having asked Doc the very same questions. "I talked to Doc. He couldn't really tell me if Brandon would recover or when. He did say

---

it might be you in danger that would trigger his memory."

Hagen snorted. "Like that will happen. If he's not around me, then how can he?" She rose, paced to the window and parted the sheers to stare out. "I'm moving back to my place, Brennen. I'll move my shop as well as soon as I can get my building redone."

"That's not necessary, Hagen. You're more than welcome to stay here and to keep your shop here."

She didn't respond. Brennen finally rose, his eyes on the fingers he has rubbing together, before he turned and walked away, anger rising in him. Anger directed at the men responsible. Anger directed at life in general. And anger directed at Brandon. He hoped he didn't meet him in the hallway. He just might help Brandon's memory along, and that wasn't what he needed to do. He prayed for the anger to disappear, prayed that Brandon would remember Hagen and the girls.

Hagen turned when Brennen had left, heading for her bedroom to pack her clothes and then to the office to pack what she had there. She hesitated in the twins' room but resolutely packed their belongings, carting everything down to her van, and realizing they really didn't have that much. Not any more. She stood for a moment, her eyes directed to where her shop was, and then slipped into the van, pulling away, not looking backwards. If she had, she would have seen Brandon standing there, staring after her, a puzzled look on his face. And she would have been Brady watching both of them, before he shook his head and

—

went to find Fynn, wrapping her in his arms, holding her as she wept for her friends.

Haley and Holly positioned themselves in the van, chattering away, telling Hagen about their day at school, before they realized they were heading to their own home.

"Hagen? Why are we going this way?" Holly turned to stare back at her sister.

"We're moving back to the house, girls. It's what we have to do."

"But Hagen? What about Brandon?" Haley waited for her sister to answer, not sure about what she was saying

Hagen didn't respond, simply drove to their home, and parked, before she opened the back of the van and began pulling out their luggage. Haley and Holly reached for theirs, once more exchanging glances.

Later that evening, the twins approached Hagen, finding her seating on the couch in the office, where they used to gather with their father and mother, to hear him read their devotions and then pray for them. They looked over at each other, before they wrapped their arms around Hagen.

Hagen stirred, almost asleep when they came in, the pain in her ribs and abdomen less than the pain in her heart.

"Hagen? What happened?" Holly started the questions.

"What about Brandon? Does he know where we are?"

Hagen shrugged. "I'm sorry, girls. I'm just so sorry. Brandon doesn't remember us. To him, we're strangers. I can't stay there. I'm so sorry." The tears she had been resolutely holding back began to flow, the looks on the girls' faces opening the flood gates.

Arms around each other, the sisters grieved and then sat in silence.

"Why doesn't he remember?" Holly was trying to puzzle it out.

"I guess when he was knocked unconscious, he ended up with amnesia. He has forgotten the last three months. I just couldn't stay there. He doesn't know who you are."

Haley sat back, determination on her face. "We'll make him remember."

"No, Haley, we don't. We live it alone. I guess it just wasn't meant to be." Hagen looked at the clock, fatigue weighing her down.. "I think we all need an early night. Head off for bed, girls. We'll need to start sorting through the shop in the morning."

"The shop? Aren't you keeping the new one?"

Hagen shrugged. "Brennen said I likely could, but I just can't go there. I'll have to start over again, girls. All over." She rose abruptly, heading for her bedroom, the door closing quietly behind her.

Haley and Holly stared at one another, not sure what to say. They both quietly rose, tidied the kitchen from their simple meal, and then headed for bed, thoughts and plots and plans running through both their brains.

Chapter 18

Three weeks had passed, with Hagen no closer to finding out what Brandon really thought. She avoided him whenever she thought they would be in contact. The twins were watching, ready to step in to help but whenever they approached Hagen about it, she had just walked away.

She didn't tell them of the increasing threats she was receiving, making her desperate to find somewhere to send them where they would be safe, but not knowing of anywhere. She had worked tirelessly on her shop, ignoring the fatigue and the pain she felt, the insurance adjuster lending advice but not questioning why she was determined to set up again in the old shop when he knew she had one all set up on the Foundation grounds. She had slipped in early one morning, early enough that no one in the building was around. The security guard on duty had been surprised when she asked for help, but shrugging, had done just that, her paperwork packed in boxes and loaded into her van. Once more, she drove away, this time for good, she thought, not seeing Brandon standing staring after her again, a puzzled look on his face.

Brandon was no closer to remembering Hagen or the girls. He would just look at anyone who commented to him about them, often turning his back and walking away. He avoided the conference room, where once he would have been in the thick of the research the others were doing. To him, she was a stranger, and at that, not one he would ever likely get to know. He ignored the niggling in his heart, that said she was his lady and he should be taking care of her.

Barnabas appeared in her shop doorway one day, startling Hagen. He didn't say anything, just walked around, studying her set up.

"Hagen? How are you feeling?" He finally perched on a stool, his eyes thoughtful as he watched her shuffle the papers on her desk.

"I don't know how I'm supposed to feel. Physically I am still healing. I shouldn't be working, I was told not to, but I don't have a choice, Barnabas. I am the sole provider for the twins. I have to start saving for their further education. This has set that plan back a long way." She raised a hand as his mouth opened. "No, don't say it. I will not accept any further assistance from the Foundation. You did too much."

Barnabas merely shrugged. "It was the Board, Hagen. They still want you to use the shop. That I have been told."

"I can't." Her voice was barely a whisper. "I can't, Barnabas. In fact, I am thinking of packing up and moving from here next year when the twins graduate. I can't stay in this town. The memories that were good are gone. All I have are bad memories."

Barnabas nodded. "I see. Talk to me again before you make a final decision. The men and the ladies tell me you and the twins are missed, but they understand. Alice said she's been in touch with you, but you're not saying much."

"Quit prying, Barnabas. I won't talk. Not to anyone." She looked down, her attention back on her work.

He watched for a moment before he rose, his heart breaking for her and also for Brandon. Now, Brandon, he thought, he's walking around lost, and I guess he's entitled, but he's hurting and he's hurting these three ladies. Lord, how do we do this?

Chapter 19

That night, Brandon shot upright in bed, his heart pounding, fear coursing through him. He didn't know why. He sprang from his bed, rapidly dressing, glad he had been able to set the crutches and then the cane aside.

He ran for his vehicle, speeding away, leaving dust in his trail that drifted into the dark night. He had no idea where he was heading before he slowed to a stop in a subdivision in town, his eyes on the darkened house in front of him.

Brandon slipped from his truck, closing the door softly before he walked rapidly up the driveway and then around the house. Something was off, he thought, but just what. He didn't see the dark form that tackled him, taking him down, a hard fist to his jaw sending his head back to hit heavily on the lawn. His only thought was he was tired of this, but just why he thought that, he had no idea. His attacker stood over him for a moment before making his way to the back door. A few movements and the lock was jimmied, the door open. He paced through the house, his eyes studying the closed doors. He had been in there before, scoping out the rooms. He knew exactly what he had to do and who he had to get.

Quietly opening the door, he slipped inside, standing for a moment to accustom himself to the dim light before he approached the bed, a cloth soaked in

93

chloroform in his hand. He slapped it over the young lady's face, combatting her struggles until they stopped. He scooped her up into his arms and paced back through the house and then outside, paced towards the back of the yard where his vehicle waited. He dumped her into the back seat, a blanket thrown over her, before he was behind the wheel and driving away. She would be his ace in the hole, he thought, one that would bring Hagen to her knees.

Hagen rose the next morning, knocking on the twins' doors as she walked down the hallway, before standing staring at the open back door. It had been locked when she went to bed. Now, how did it get open? She stepped through it onto the back patio, not seeing anything.

She sighed. Not again, Lord. Why do these things happen to me? I just want to live my life and get on with my business, get the girls through high school and then college. At that point, I can move somewhere out in the country, where I can live my life out in peace.

Pulling into the driveway, the responding officer studied Brandon's truck before he ran the plates, surprise on his face. Why would he be here, he wonder? He headed around to the back, meeting Hagen as she stood on the patio, worry on her face.

"Hagen? Talk to me. Tell me what you found."

"That." She responded, her finger pointing at the door. "That was open this morning. I distinctly remembering locking it last night."

—

"Okay. The twins? Would they have been up and about all ready?"

Hagen shook her head. "Their doors were closed when I came out." She frowned. "But they should be up. We had plans for today."

"Okay. How be you go get them up while I take a look around?" Donny Ellis paused. "Brandon's truck is on the street."

Hagen stared past him before she shrugged. "I have no idea why. He shouldn't be here." She spun on her heels, finding Haley standing in the kitchen, staring at the open door.

"Hagen, what is going on? Why is there a police officer here." She started to move past her sister until a hand on her arm stopped her.

"The door was open this morning and it seems we have had a break in." She looked around. "Where's Holly? Isn't she up?"

"No. That's unusual. She's always up before me." Haley spun on her heel, running for her sister's door, knocking and then opening it to look in. There was no sign of Holly. Haley quickly searched the room and then stood in the hallway, peering towards the single bathroom in the house. The door stood open, just as it had when she had left it moments earlier.

"Hagen!"

Hagen spun at the fear in her sister's voice, moving quickly to find her, an arm around her.

"Haley?"

"Holly! She's not here! Where is she?"

Hagen's face grew grim as she too searched her sister's room before, an arm around Haley, she rushed from the house, searching for Donnie, finding him helping Brandon to his feet.

"Brandon?" Haley's questioning voice drew his attention to her, and he shook off Donnie's hands, his own hand rubbing at his chin.

He walked slowly towards the two ladies, his eyes on Hagen's face before he looked at Haley.

"Haley? Are you okay?"

"But wait. You don't remember us."

"I guess I did forget you for a bit, but I do remember you now. Hagen?"

Hagen just shook her head, unable to speak, tears sparkling in her eyes before he swept her into his arms.

"Hagen? What's wrong?"

"It's Holly. She's missing."

Brandon stared down at her head before he swept her up into his arms, moving to seat in one of the white wicker chairs she had at the back of the house, shaking his head at Haley's comment that they would be wet. He watched Haley for a moment, standing forlorn, her face covered with tears, fear shaking her body before he reached out an arm and motioned her over, sweeping her into a hug as well. His arms encircled the two ladies, his eyes on Donnie, who had approached as he heard Hagen's voice.

"Donnie, can you check? They say Holly is missing."

Donnie nodded, his hand going to his service weapon, as he entered the house, to move through it quickly, to stop beside Holly's bed, his eyes on the discarded rag on the floor. Even now, the faint odour of chloroform hung in the air near it. He shook his head, walking rapidly outside, grabbing a blanket from the living room and draping it around Hagen and Haley before he walked away, dismay on his face. He had been a schoolmate of Hagen's and considered her a good friend. His wife, Annie, had been one of her close friends for years.

Chapter 20

Will stood, his head bowed as he listened to the report Donnie was giving, before he nodded.

"No signs of her around at all?"

"No, sir. We've searched the house and the shop. There's a crawl space, but it hasn't been disturbed. Hagen said she rarely goes down there, other than to check on the plumbing and the venting pipes. She opens the windows in the spring and in fact, just closed them up last night." Donnie looked around as he heard a vehicle pull to a stop. "There's Barnabas and Brendon. And Baird. And Buckley."

Will gave a quick grin. "I called Baird. Looks as if he brought reinforcements with him. I'm glad Buckley is here." Will peered towards the back of the house, watching Brandon and Hagen from where he stood. "We need to get them away from there."

Donnie nodded. "I know. Hagen has just refused to leave. I did get Haley to move to my car." He ducked to look through the window. "She's hurting, Will."

"I know. Those two girls are close, but what they went through losing their parents have made them even closer." Will walked towards Brandon. "Brandon? Can we talk?"

Brandon nodded, moving away from Hagen, feeling he was deserting her.

—

"Will? Any news?"

"Not that I am aware. Listen, we need to get Hagen and Haley out of here. The team is going to be here for a while. I can't let them back into the house." He squinted at the sky. "It's going to rain soon." He looked down to see Hagen standing in front of him, Haley with her arm around her sister.

"Will? Have you news?" Hagen was hopeful, but doubtful at the same time.

"No, I'm sorry, Hagen. I don't. Listen, I need to move you and Haley out of here. The team is going to be a while. Let Brandon take you back to the Foundation building."

Hagen sighed. "I just left there, you know."

Will gave a swift grin. "I know you did, but right now, that's where I need you to be. I know you were attacked there, and I know I am repeating my "I knows"." He grinned at Haley for a moment before sobering. "At least there, we have security that we can place with you."

Hagen turned to Haley, studying her sister, seeing the devastation in her face. "It's my fault, Will. If I hadn't come back, Holly wouldn't be missing."

"No, I don't think you're correct. We've heard rumours on the streets that someone has been following the twins. We just didn't have enough information to identify who it was. So, it wouldn't have mattered where you were. One of them would have still be taken. If they had been together, the other one may well have been injured."

Hagen had paled at his words, her arm tightening around Haley. "Then I guess we must." She turned to the house, intending on packing for them, when his hand stopped her.

"I'm sorry, Hagen. I can't let you go into the house. The ladies will make sure you have what you need." Will was apologetic but firm.

"Thank you. I wasn't thinking." She looked towards the shop. "If you can, there are some boxes with patterns and designs. Can you retrieve those for me? I take it we won't be back here for a while."

"No, I don't think you will. We'll look after getting those for you. Right now, we need you two to go with Brandon. Brandon, leave your keys. We'll get your truck to you. Barnabas is here. You can go with one of them."

Barnabas watched Brandon walk towards him, simply opening his vehicle door for Hagen and Haley to seat themselves before he threw a questioning look at Brandon.

"Brandon? What is going on? And where is Holly?"

"And why are you here?" This from Buckley.

"I was awakened in the night, feeling a fear for someone. I don't remember driving here but I didn't recognize the house. I walked around the house to check things out and got clobbered again. That removed the block to my memory." He looked down, momentarily overcome with his emotions. "It's Holly. She's missing. Their back door was broken in and she disappeared. Will said they found evidence that she was taken from her bed.”

His words shocked the four men standing beside him, Buckley stepping back so he could watch Hagen and Haley.

“Let’s get them home.” Brendon spoke quietly. “I’ll go find some of the ladies and take them shopping for the three of them.”

“Do that, Brendon. Keep your bills and submit them.” Barnabas turned back to watch the activity. “What about her shop?”

“She hadn’t unpacked, I guess. Will said he’d get the boxes for her. And he’ll make sure my truck gets to me.” Brandon slipped into the seat beside Hagen, an arm around her shoulders, his hand resting on Haley, who leaned into it.

Chapter 21

Pacing the living room of the apartment she was once more back in, Hagen listened to the quiet conversation from the office and from the kitchen. Will had officers there, equipment in place to trace the call when it came. Hagen had snorted at that, drawing his eyes to her face.

"I doubt they'll call. They'll wait until I'm outside and just walk up to me. Can you prevent that?" She walked away from him before he could answer.

Haley watched her sister from where she had plopped herself down in a chair when they had entered the apartment, not moving, wishing it had been herself instead of Holly. Why, God? Why did you let it happen? Why Holly? Why here? She finally just wrapped her arms around her upraised knees and buried her face against them, not wanting anyone to see that she was weeping.

Brandon watched from the doorway before he moved towards Hagen. Sensing him near her, she turned and then walked into his embrace, his arms tight around her.

"Brandon, what am I to do? I need to find my sister."

"I know, darlin'. I know. Will's working on it. The guys are all in the conference room, working away. Fynn has called a friend who does searches on people. She's working on that."

Hagen nodded. "But who? My business isn't one that you can just take over. I don't ship on a regular basis, if that's what they're after. So why?"

"That's what we're trying to determine." He drew her down to the couch, his arm tight around her, a nod of thanks to Berneen, Baird's wife, who brought in a tray with hot drinks for them, and then stayed, her arm around Haley, as she perched on the chair arm.

"Who would do this?" Hagen looked up as she heard footsteps, and Burnie appeared, sinking down onto the coffee table in front of her. "Burnie?"

"Hagen, it's okay. I just have some questions, questions that arose as we were researching."

She nodded, watching as Haley's head raised, her heart breaking for her young sister.

"Okay. Your father, what did he do for a living?"

She told him, described what her mother had done, and then what had happened to them. She paused, a thought running through her mind, a thought that dismayed her but also scared her.

Brandon picked up on her emotions. "Hagen, what did you just think about?"

She turned to face him, her eyes haunted. "The man that hit them. He was drunk. The bar he had been at was charged for allowing him to drink over the limit. The bartender threatened us. I had forgotten that, tucked it away back in my mind. The bar owner didn't stop the threats, but I often wondered if he felt the same way. He lost his business because of that. The twins and I wouldn't sue. It wouldn't have brought Mom and Dad back. I have seen him around town, catching him watching me at times, and I have wondered what his mindset was."

Burnie nodded. "That's what we're looking for, Hagen. Thank you. Now, with your father's work, did he have any enemies that you know of?"

Hagen shrugged, her eyes on Haley. "There was one of family that accused Dad of being biased and of doing shoddy, negligent work, but he hadn't. An investigation proved he had done everything as it should be done. You and Holly were about six or seven at the time, I think, Haley. Dad and Mom wouldn't talk much about it, but there is always the possibility that a grudge hung on." She reached for the pad of paper and pen that Burnie offered her, writing down that name and any other name she could think of. She looked up to see Dallas standing behind Burnie. "Burnie, Dallas is here. Can you give him a copy of that?"

"I can." Burnie stood, an apology on his lips that was never uttered as Dallas shook his head.

"It's okay, Burnie. You're asking the questions I would of Hagen and that I have of others." He stabbed a finger towards the paper. "Just give me a copy of that. On second thought, I'll just take a photo of it." His phone was out of his pocket as he spoke, the photo taken and his phone tucked away. He looked towards Hagen, his eyes catching Brandon watching her, his heart on his face. "Anything else, Hagen?"

She shook her head, her emotions in too much of a roil to clearly think or speak. "Just find my Holly." Her head went down on Brandon's shoulder and her eyes closed, even though she didn't sleep. Her mind drifted to years past and stayed there as her memories filled her with joy and sorrow.

I don't know who, Lord, but You do. Please, dear Lord, protect our Holly. Bring her back safe to us. Don't this haunt any of us for years to come. Hagen heard Brandon's prayer before her emotions took over and sent her into a sleep, a sleep she desperately needed but wanted to avoid.

Haley watched her sister, a woebegone look on her face. She huddled in her chair, tears on her face, as Brandon looked up. A movement of his arm had Haley flying to him, to be tucked up close to the man that she had begun to think of as her brother. She heard his prayer for her and for Holly before she too slept, her emotions overtaking her, just as they had with her sister.

Brandon looked up as he heard footsteps, and Will appeared followed by Barnabas. Both men sank wearily into chairs.

Brandon studied Will before he spoke.

"Any word?" He kept his voice low, not wanting to disturb the ladies he held tight to his heart.

Will nodded. "There is. We have sighting of the man who we think is involved. Plainclothes men are following him, ready to move in. We had word from the street about a possible hideaway for him." He sighed as he reached for his phone. Some days, he regretted being the chief of police. Today was one of them.

As he listened, his eyes shot towards Hagen and then Haley, before he was on his feet, almost running from the room, his voice calling for Dallas, who ran after him.

"Will?" Dallas paused at the foot of the stairs, waiting for Will to finish his conversation and pocket his phone.

"Thank the good Lord, they found her. She's still out, from what they said. Brady was the paramedic on call. Thank God for that. She knows him, if she awakes."

"We need to tell Hagen."

"And we will. Right now, they're working on removing her from the building she was in."

"Will? I don't like the sounds of that."

"No, I don't either. It's booby-trapped and they've made their way to her. It took time for them to clear a pathway. They'll bring her out and then bring her here. Doc has asked for that. I can't see the harm in it. If we take her to the hospital, they'll find her there."

"That they will." Dallas paced. "We need to awaken Hagen."

"We will, Dallas. We will. Once we have Holly here, we'll go get her."

Chapter 22

Rousing, Holly looked around, a frown on her face, fear suddenly hitting her. This was not her bedroom, and it was late in the day, she could tell, just from the way the sun shone through the window. She raised herself up, staring at her nightclothes before she looked up, her face relaxing as she saw Doc.

"Doc? Where am I? I'm not at home."

"No, you're not, young Holly. How are you feeling? About like that. What I would expect. I just need to listen to your heart and lungs and then Will and Dallas want to talk to you."

"But where am I?"

"You're in the infirmary at the Foundation building. You went on an adventure and didn't ask any of us to come with you." He grinned as she frowned at him.

"I don't remember. Why not?"

"Because, young lady, you were chloroformed." Doc stepped back. "You're fine, just sleepy, I suspect. Now, here are Will and Dallas."

Dallas approached, a smile on his face that didn't quite reach his eyes. He was not used to talking to teenagers.

"Holly, Doc says you're fine. Do you remember anything at all about today?"

Holly shook her head. "No, I don't. I remember going to bed last night. We had planned to go for a hike this morning, I think it was. Just the three of us. Hagen said we needed some our time." She looked up at Dallas. "What happened? Why am I here?"

"You were chloroformed and taken from your bedroom sometime early this morning. We were searching for you, found out where you were and brought you here. You don't remember waking up at all?"

She shook her head, her eyes closing for a moment against the headache that had begun to pound at her temples and behind her eyes. "No, I don't. Can I see Hagen and Haley, please?"

Dallas shared a look with Doc, who nodded. "We can do that. Here, this is what we're going to do. I'm just going to pick you up and carry you to your apartment here. Hagen and Haley are waiting there for you."

"I'm glad we're back here. I like it here." Her head went down on his shoulder and she slept. Dallas tilted his head to look at her before sharing a look with Doc.

"It will take time to get out of her system. I don't know how much she was given, but she was either given a lot or else her system can't handle it. She shouldn't have still be sleeping when she was found. It was hours."

"I know, Doc. Let's move. I have two ladies who need to see this young lady." Dallas walked away, his concentration on getting Holly to her siblings, not seeing the men and ladies from the building who had gathered in the lobby at the news, relief and joy on their faces, prayers on their lips.

Doc opened the door for Dallas and then held it as Dallas entered, his eyes watchful that he didn't hit either Holly's feet or head. Brandon looked up at the sound of the footsteps, his eyes widening as he saw Holly. Doc pointed to the other couch in the living room.

"Right there." His voice was low and he reached for a blanket to cover her. "How long have they been sleeping, Brandon?"

He squinted at his watch. "About an hour." He felt Hagen stirring, her eyes opening before she looked up at him, a frown on her face.

"Brandon? Where are we?"

"In the apartment, Hagen. I have someone here who I think you want to see."

She frowned again, before she shook her heard. "I don't know who that would be."

"It's Holly, Hagen. She's here and she's safe."

Brandon watched as her beloved face continued to hold a frown before she sat upright, frantically looking around before she saw her sister. She was out of Brandon's arms and on her knees beside Holly, a shaking hand reaching out to touch her hair and then her face before her arm was around her sister and her face against her as almost silent sobs shook her body.

Haley roused next, blinking in the soft lamplight before she noticed Hagen was not there.

"Hagen?" She looked around, finding Dallas standing nearby, a smile on his face. "Dallas? Any word? I dreamt she was here."

"This time, your dream is true." He stepped back just enough so she could see Hagen on her knees. "Holly's home, Haley."

Haley sat, her mouth open, shock on her face before she scrambled to escape the blanket she had been covered with, tripping on it as her feet entangled in it with her rush to get to her sisters. She was beside Hagen, arms around both of her sisters as much as she could, sobs shaking her as well.

The men watched, compassion on their faces, before Brandon rose and pointed to the kitchen.

"Dallas. How?"

"I can't go into all the details, but we had been watching someone. Word from the street reached us as to a possible place where she was held. The ERT went in and brought her out." Dallas paused. "Brady is the one who took the call. Don't ask him. He can't and won't say much."

"I won't." Brandon took the mug of coffee that he had been handed, stepping back to stare into the living room. "I am thankful that she's here. Does she remember much that we'll have to work with?"

"No. She was never awake. It was a surprise to her to wake up downstairs." Dallas excused himself and walked away, rolling his head to try and relieve the tension in his shoulders. He still faced a long night, that much he knew.

Chapter 23

Haley watched Holly closely over the next couple of days, not willing to be away from her, to the point, Holly turned on her one day, almost angry with her.

"Haley? Can you please leave me alone?"

Haley dug in her heels, not willing to admit her fear. Buckley had heard them as he approached where they were standing outside the building, facing one another.

"Ladies? Just who I was looking for. I'm hungry for some ice cream and am heading to town. Care to join me?" He watched, biting back as a smile as the twins continued to stare at one another before Haley agreed readily, Holly more grumpily.

Sitting in the ice cream parlour, Buckley teased them, bringing smiles finally to both their faces. Buckley was a well-loved pastor to his congregation, ready with a smile, a word of Scripture, or a helping hand or listening ear.

"Holly? If you need to talk, let me know. I listen really good, I'm told." Buckley grinned as she stared at him, her mouth open.

"It's really well.   Don't you know your grammar?" She stared at him as he just continued to grin. "You did that on purpose."

He shrugged, watching Haley for a moment, before he sobered.

"Ladies, I know this has been tough on you both, in different ways. Don't let it come between you." He held up a hand at Haley's protest. "I know, Haley. You're afraid Holly will disappear again, this time for good. Holly doesn't understand how worried and scared you were. Just be patient with one another. Let each other have space like you used to." He grinned again as they stared at him, gathering up the debris from their treat. "How'd I do?"

"You nailed it perfectly." Holly bit at her lip. "I'm sorry, Haley. I didn't understand. And I should have. We're twins. We're supposed to know these things about one another."

"It's okay. I've been hovering, afraid you will disappear."

Buckley stood later and watched as Brandon walked towards him, a spring in his step for a change.

"Buckley? You waiting for me?" Brandon grinned, his whole face alight

"I am. Have you and Hagen set a date yet?"

Brandon shook his head. "Not yet, but we're talking about that. Why? You have a date available?"

Buckley just grinned. "I do. Let's see if you pick the same one." He looked around, then down at the envelope he held. "Listen. I found this envelope today outside Hagen's shop. She hadn't been around there, I don't think."

"No, she hadn't been. She had had some appointments to go to. What is it?"

"There was no name on it, so I opened it. It's a death threat, Brandon, directed at Hagen. How do we keep her safe? The guys are working as hard as they can to figure it out but are running into road blocks."

Brandon, who had been back to work, nodded. "That's what I have been hearing. Someone is deliberately blocking information. And I think I know who. I just don't have the proof I need." He said a name, Buckley staring at him in surprise, then consternation.

"Them? It makes sick sense, do you know that? Come on. Let's start our search. And I want to pass that on to Emma Finlay. We also need to pass this on to Dallas."

Brandon nodded. "We do. How do we stay safe, Buckley. They've proven that they can get into our building, into their home. Just how do we do that?"

"Prayer for one thing. Another thing is to get you two married. It may help but it may not. Whoever it is has proven they really don't care who gets hurt."

"And that is what bothers me. Someone innocent will be hurt."

"I know." Buckley held the entrance door open, waiting for Brandon to walk through, stopping short as he saw Hagen waiting for them.

Hagen walked towards them and in the arms that Brandon held open for her. He could feel her trembling.

———

"Hagen?"

"The twins have been threatened again. I can't do this, Brandon. I need to keep them safe, but how do I do just that when I have no idea who is after me. Or what they even want."

"They want revenge, Hagen. Come, over here to one of the sitting areas." Buckley pointed to one of the two areas on either side of the lobby that had been set up with couches, chairs, tables and a gas fireplace. "We need to talk. I found an envelope near your shop, with a death threat directed at you. Dallas is on his way out, when he can get here."

"The girls? They want to start riding the bus, but I'm afraid to let them."

"No, that's not a good idea. For now, let us take care of getting them back and forth. The guys have all volunteered to do just that."

"I can't thank them enough."

They talked for a while longer before Buckley excused himself and walked away, a meeting hanging over his head. Brandon watched him before he turned to Hagen.

"Hagen? We need to set a date."

"I know." She sounded grumpy and then sighed, apologizing to him. "I just wish Mom and Dad were here, but wishes doesn't make that happen." She turned her face up to him, surprised as he reached to kiss her and then kiss her again. "Brandon? We're supposed to be planning."

"I know. I'm planning on how I can sneak another kiss." With that said, he reached down and kissed her again. "Okay. So, planning it is. Any thoughts as to dates?'

She nodded. "I talked to the girls. None of us want me to have a big fancy wedding. That's just not me."

"No, but we need to have one we can look back on and cherish as the first step in our married life. Threats aside, we need to move forward." He pulled out his phone and brought up his calendar. "I see I have this Saturday free."

"Well, isn't that a coincidence. I just happen to as well." She leaned into his hug. "And Buckley was dropping hints. He said he was free Saturday as well. Would it do?"

Brandon shouted with laughter, startling Hagen for a moment, and drawing the twins towards them, just as they had entered the building.

"He did that with both Brady and Fynn and Branigan and Guenivere. One of these days, it will backfire and it will be his turn to be asked that."

The twins shared a look before Holly hesitantly spoke.

"Hagen? What's going on?"

"How about this Saturday for the wedding? Will it work for you?"

Brandon sat back as he listened to the excited chatter from the twins and the calm voice of his sweetheart. Yes, Lord, I hear. I am willing to go

———

forward as is Hagen. Please, though, Lord, keep my lady and her sisters safe. Help Dallas to find out whoever this is and soon. None of the three can take much more.

Chapter 24

Two weeks later, Hagen stood in her shop, staring down at the wedding band on her finger and the beautiful emerald stone in her engagement ring. She was happy, content, she thought, except for whoever it was after her. She had had more emails come to her business account, each more and more vicious. Dallas had sent them on to the lab, shaking his head, saying that they would try and track them but the lab was backlogged at the moment. He could not say when they would be looked at.

She looked around as the door opened and then began to back away. She knew this man. Her father had had dealings with him and had warned her about him.

"Well, Hagen. I see we are finally alone. Just how I planned it." He walked towards her, his overweight body heavy on his feet. "We need to have a chat."

"We have nothing to talk about. Now, please, leave." Hagen retreated behind the reception counter, her fingers feeling for the button she knew was there.

"Not until we come to an understanding, my dear. Your business is just what I need. Your dolls and wood crafts are perfect." He picked up one of her display dolls, turning the wooden toy over and over in his hands.

"No, I don't see how they would be perfect for you. You have no family."

"That's correct. However, these dolls can be hollowed out very easily. Drugs that I supply will go inside and you will ship them to where I tell you to. If you are reluctant to do that, I would hate to see something happen to one of your sisters."

"It was you, wasn't it? You're the one behind it. But now, you don't have the smarts for that." She was taunting him, desperate to delay him until help could arrive, if it ever did. "Dad always said someone smarter was behind you." She looked up at that point, her face blanching as she did so.

He reached for her, pulling her across the counter, sending anything on it flying, before he slammed her against it again and again. She collapsed when he let go, to huddle on the floor, the pain that was wracking her body taking every cohesive thought from her mind. She couldn't understand his words, only vaguely saw him walking away and then heard the door slamming behind him. She sank into a dark well of pain, not hearing the door fly open and the security guard dropping to his knees beside her, his phone out calling for help.

Brandon stood beside Barnabas and Brody, who had their hands on his shoulders, holding him in place, his eyes glued to the activity going on around his wife's shop. He had just arrived home from work when he saw the activity and feared the worse.

"I need to get there, Brody. I need to know Hagen is okay." Desperation laced his words.

"You can't, Brandon. You just can't. We'll get you to her, but they need to work on her." Brody shared a look with Barnabas who turned and walked away, searching for Dallas.

"Dallas? What's the word?"

"The security guard isn't sure what happened, but he said Hagen was attacked. The paramedics are working on her." Dallas was frustrated. "Can't I ever have a straightforward investigation with your guys?"

Barnabas cracked a grim smile. "I wish they didn't have to go through what they did but they have. God has allowed it. We just need to figure out who." He turned as he heard his name called. "What do you have, Joe?"

"This. We caught a picture of him as he was stalking around the buildings. I know him. He's high in the world of drugs."

Dallas and Barnabas shared a look. "This makes horrible sense, doesn't it, Dallas? Her handcrafts would be the perfect carrier for them. Who would think of toys?"

"True, but there is something else. What has happened doesn't just fit one person. Did she have to have two involved?" Dallas walked away, leaving Barnabas staring after him.

"Did he really say two parties?" Breck spoke from beside him

Barnabas turned, to find most of the men, except for Brody and Brandon, standing near him. "He did, and I think he's right. We've been focusing on one.

But there are two. Let's see what we can come up with." He handed the photo to Blair. "Here, run with this. He's a nasty piece of work. He's the one who assaulted her today."

Seeing the stretcher moving towards him, Brandon broke from Brody's hand on his shoulder and almost ran towards it. He slid to a halt, his eyes on Hagen's white, pain-filled face.

"What happened to her?"

"Her back is injured, that's all we know for now." The paramedic shared a look with Brady, who had moved closer. "We need to get her to help, Brandon. Brady?"

"I'll get him there. Go on, fellows." Brady's hand kept Brandon beside him. "Come with me, Brandon. We'll head it. Brendon and Benen are heading for the twins."

Brandon nodded, almost too numb to comprehend what he has being told, heading for Brady's truck, Fynn holding the back door open for him. She watched him closely before exchanging a glance with Brady. Once they arrived at the hospital, he paced the waiting room, his eyes not leaving the doors to the examination rooms. He was anxious, distraught, he just didn't know what word to use for himself. He was sure Burnie could come up with a few, if he asked him.

Doc paused for a moment before he pushed open the doors, not wanting to talk with Brandon but knowing he had no choice. He knew the twins had arrived, word had got back to him. Why, Lord? Why?

———

I know You're in control, but why Hagen? The twins need her. Brandon and she are just starting a life together. I shouldn't be having to go out and tell a young husband that I don't know how damaged his wife's back is, that I don't if she is permanently injured or not. Sometimes, Lord, life just is not fair.

He stood, his eyes on Brandon, before he looked around the waiting room, a small smile crossing his face. Yes, it was what he had expected. The Foundation building family, that was growing couple by couple, were all there, surrounding Brandon, comforting the twins, who saw him and were on their feet, running towards him. Doc just opened his arms and swept them close. He and Anna had taken over as grandparents for them.

Brandon spun as he caught movement from the corner of his eye, seeing the twins moving towards Doc. His own feet took him that way, reluctant in part, but knowing he had to talk with his friend. He stopped short of Doc, a question on his face that he didn't want to ask, but knew he had to.

Chapter 25

His hand raising to grip Brandon's shoulder, Doc then pointed to the outside doors, his arms still around the twins.

"Let's walk, Brandon, girls. I need some fresh air. And a break. It's been a bad day all around." Doc didn't tell them that he had lost a young mother and her infant to a motor vehicle accident, despite the best efforts of all involved. Then to have a friend appear as Hagen had, with questionable long-term injuries, he just didn't know how to cope for a moment.

"Doc?" Brandon paced beside him as they headed towards the picnic table under the trees.

Doc sank down, a sigh wrenched from him, a twin sticking close to either side of him. He watched as Brandon sat across from him, seeing some of the men from the building gathering close.

"Brandon. Haley. Holly. Hagen is alive, thank God for that. From what I understand and can see, it could easily have been a funeral home we were gathering in." He watched as the girls' faces whitened with fear. "That being said, we still have unknowns that we are investigating and then determining treatment. How much were you told, Brandon?"

"Not much, other than she was assaulted. Doc, I know you. What aren't you telling us?"

Doc nodded, moving his arms so he could clasp his hands together, raising his eyes to search for Buckley, who stood close by.

"Buckley? Will you pray for these three and for Hagen?"

Buckley nodded, slipping to the bench seat beside Brandon, an arm resting across his friend's shoulders as he prayed, asking for healing for Hagen, for wisdom of the medical staff, for release of fear from the three with him.

Doc raised his head when Buckley had finished, the verse coming to mind of the woman with the issue who had been healed simply by touching the Master's garment hem.

"Brandon. It seems that Hagen was repeated shoved against the counter in her shop. I can't tell you how many times. I doubt she even knows. At the moment, she's in imaging, for X-rays. And whatever else we may need to do. An MRI is likely as well. Her kidneys are badly bruised from this assault. How serious is it? We don't know. We do know there is a lot of swelling around the spine. That will go down. Until it does, we won't know if there is any permanent damage." He reached to hug Haley as he heard her start to sob. Fynn, he knew, had seated herself near Holly, an arm around her.

"Doc? Permanent? As she would be crippled?" At Doc's nod, Brandon's eyes slid shut, sorrow gripping him before anger took over. "How long before we know?"

"That I can't tell you. It will take time, days, weeks, I can't say for sure. The swelling needs to go down. As of tonight, she is still reacting to sensory touching on her feet and legs, but the swelling will get worse."

"Can we see her?" Holly's voice was barely above a whisper, choked with tears as it was.

"You can. Head back into the waiting room. I need to see whereabouts she is a present. I'm sending her up to a room as soon as I can."

Doc stood and walked away, Blair, Brendon and Breck meeting him.

"Doc?" Blair's voice held a question.

"It's not great, fellows. She may be crippled. Right now, we need to deal with those three. And find whoever the monster is who did this." Anger laced Doc's words, anger he knew he would have to ask forgiveness for.

"We're working on that, Doc. We have a picture of the man who did this. Dallas has sent it out to all the patrol vehicles. They want this over for Hagen and the twins." Breck's voice had a bite to it.

"Good. Now, I'm heading in there." Doc pointed at the door, before pointing back over his shoulder. "You stay with them. If whoever it is can't get to Hagen, he'll go after one of them. And I can almost guarantee you, this maniac was not working on his own."

Brandon stood, his arms around the twins, at Hagen's bedside an hour or so later. She had been moved to a private room, at Barnabas' insistence. He studied her, seeing her laying on her side, foam bolsters behind her back to keep her from rolling to that position. He traced her beloved face with his eyes, seeing the pain that it held, pain not relieved by the medications she had been given.

Holly hugged him, her head against him, her tears wetting his shirt. Haley hugged him as well, but she was not weeping. Not that showed, but he figured she was weeping inside. Each twin had their own way of dealing with this. All he could do, he thought, was be there for them, and pray for them.

Haley's hand reached to touch her sister's hair, just a light touch, not wanting to cause any more pain.

"Brandon? What is Doc is right? What if it is permanent?" Holly's question did not surprise him.

"Then, we deal with that at the time. Only God knows, love, and that's not a trite, off-the-cuff remark. He really is in control of this." He watched for a moment, before the twins walked away, leaving him on his own. He moved closer to his beloved bride, a hand on hers and the other hand on her face, wishing it was him and not her it had happened to.

Hagen's eyes flickered for a moment before she groaned.

"Brandon? Are you there? And just where is there?"

He gave a slight grin at the nonsensical way she was speaking, knowing it was the pain and the medications doing it.

125

"I'm right here, darlin'. And this is the hospital. You were hurt."

"I know. It was Barney Soles who did it. Dad had run-ins with him all the time. He warned me about him." She stopped speaking, the pain taking her voice for a moment. "What did he do?"

"He apparently slammed you into the reception counter. You have an injury to your back and kidneys."

"He was vicious, Brandon. He wanted to use my handcrafts to smuggle drugs. I can't let him do that. I'll close down before I do." Tears sparkled on her cheeks, tears of pain and fear and frustration, that Brandon reached to wipe away.

Brandon bent over the bed, his arm around his lady as he prayed, watching as she drifted off to sleep, a kiss dropped on her temple, before he stood upright, anger burning deeper inside him, before he prayed, asking for the anger to be removed and for the peace that only God could give. He didn't want to see Hagen give up her dream, but he knew she would if she had to.

He turned as he heard footsteps approaching. Breck and Bradon stood beside him.

"How is she?" Bradon's question brought through the silence in the room.

"She's hurting, Bradon, and ready to give up her dream to prevent him from using it. She named him."

"Barney Soles." Brandon stared at Bradon. "We have a picture. Weren't you told that?"

"I guess I was. There's just been too much thrown at me right now. Listen, the girls will want to stay, but I think they should head home."

"Fynn said she'd look after them. Alice is on duty, she said. If anything, Anna will step in. In fact, Anna's in the waiting room with them now."

Brandon nodded. "I'm not leaving, but I am really worried about them. I don't know how far these people will go. They have already tried by kidnapping to get Hagen to agree."

"I know." Breck looked towards the bed, his eyes doing his own assessment of both Hagen and Brandon. "We'll watch them. Fynn has suggested that you speak with their school, and have their work given to them that they can do at home or online. You know they will want to be where Hagen is."

"I know. Doc thinks she'll be here for a couple of days and then allowed home. He said he'd speak with the physician taking over her care, to see where she would stand with that."

Chapter 26

Shifting in the recliner set near Hagen's hospital bed, Brandon pulled the blanket he had been given higher up on his neck, folding his arms across his chest when he was finished, just trying to find a comfortable position, an impossible task, he finally decided. He was exhausted, but didn't want to sleep, wanted to wait for Hagen to rouse and talk to him. The nurse had been in and out over the course of the evening and into the wee small hours of the day, speaking quietly to him, finding him a coffee and a muffin from their breakroom.

He watched his bride, sorrowing because she was hurt, but with anger still burning within him. He didn't want to see her dream fail, he just didn't. But Brandon knew that was a real possibility. Hagen would just shut down her shop if she had to, putting aside what she really wanted for the sake of others.

His head turned as he hear footsteps approaching, and Barnabas appeared. Brandon glared at his watch, seeing how early it was.

"Barnabas? What are you doing here?"

"I had to come. I couldn't sleep, Brandon. Something is off about this whole thing with Hagen."

"I know. I just don't get it." Brandon looked behind him at the door and then at Hagen, as she moved restlessly, nearing time for more pain medications. "I worry about Hagen, and the twins. I talked to Dallas earlier tonight. He doesn't seem to be getting any sleep. Anyway, patrol officers found the man who assaulted her yesterday. He's in jail, but not talking. Dallas said he hasn't even asked for a lawyer yet. The charges are still being sorted out."

"It will take a while, I suspect." Barnabas reached for a chair, seating himself wearily. He was tired and worn out, needing a holiday, but refusing to go when his friends needed him. Lord, we need to get through this, and I just don't see how we will.

Hagen stirred, rousing more, the pain driving her to awake. She gave a small moan, her tongue moving over her lips, trying to moisten them. She sucked greedily at the ice chips Brandon placed in her mouth, his hand resting finally on her cheek before he bent and kissed her.

"Brandon? What time is it?"

"About three in the morning."

Hagen squinted at him. "You're still in the clothes you put on this morning. How come?"

Brandon gave a half-laugh. "I haven't had a chance to change. Somebody needed me more to stay with her."

"And who would that be?" Hagen sounded grumpy.

"You, my love. You're in the hospital again."

"I am? Why?" Her voice died away as she slipped once more into sleep, the nurse entering on almost silent shoes, ready to give the next dose of the pain medication.

"She's been awake?"

"Just briefly." Brandon waited for her to leave. "What else, Barnabas? I know you. You have something else on your mind."

Barnabas sighed. "You're right. I talked to both Will and Dallas. Even with this man arrested, Hagen is still in grave danger. Whoever it is behind it all? We think it was more than just the drugs. Somehow, someone else who her father had dealings with is involved."

"I would say they're right." Brandon bit at his lip, Hagen and he having discussed that very thing. "Hagen came up with some names, was it only a day or so ago? She couldn't sleep the night before last. I found her in the office, papers all over the place. She had been researching everyone she could remember having dealings with the family, or who she knew had threatened retaliation against her father. There is a list in the folder on the desk. Have one of the twins get it for you, or go on in and get it yourself. It's a green folder." He gave a low laugh. "Hagen wanted green. She said these men and women were envious of her father and her mother, and green was the colour of envy."

Barnabas gave a grin. "She thinks in colour, doesn't she? A true artist."

"That she is." Brandon struggled with a thought. "I think I know who we need to look into." His voice died away.

Brandon shifted in his seat, his head turning as he watched Brandon.

"Brandon?"

"I think it's Ben or someone related to him. He knew Hagen's parents. There has been something off, with him saying he had had complaints about her. That doesn't make sense."

"No, it hasn't." Barnabas pulled out his phone, jotting some some thoughts. "We'll see where we go from there."

Brandon nodded, his chin dropping, and his eyes closing as he slept. The worry about Hagen had drained him to the point that he felt he could not go on. Hagen roused at one point, her eyes on him, before shifting to the door, a frown on her face as she saw someone hovering out there. She knew that person, just wasn't sure if she was really seeing him. Her gaze shifted to Barnabas, watching him for a moment before he looked up at her, a smile on his face, that didn't quite reach his eyes.

"Hagen?" His voice was low

"Barnabas, he's here. Why is Ben outside my door?"

Barnabas was on his feet, moving that way, stepping outside before he stepped back in

"He's gone, Hagen. You're sure?"

"I am. I have never trusted him. Dad seemed to but Mom always had a hesitation about him. I trusted her instincts."

"I have someone looking into him. Brandon mentioned him. Now, how are you feeling?"

"How am I supposed to feel?" Her grumpy response brought a glimmer of a smile to his face. "I'm sorry. I am not normally like this."

Barnabas leaned against the side of the bed, his eyes staring ahead of him, a thought crossing his mind before he spoke.

"It's understandable, Hagen. You have been through a lot, in what, the last fifteen or sixteen months. Losing your parents like you did? That would be enough, but to take on raising fifteen-year-old twins at the time, when you are all grieving? Yes, I would say that has been tough. And then through into the mix what has happened now. You're entitled."

"No, I'm not. I need to leave it with God, asking for His peace in this, and I struggle with that. I struggle with the fact that I will likely have to give up my dream." Her voice died away. When she spoke again, her voice was barely audible, and he could hear the devastation in it. "I won't let my business be used like he wanted."

Chapter 27

Seated in a wheelchair, Hagen stared around the apartment, not sure what was off but she was sure something was. She pushed herself forward, pain moving through her back, but she persisted. It had been a week, she thought, since her attack. Insisting that she had to come home three days prior, she had just stared at Brandon when he protested before he held up his hands and nodded.

Brandon watched closely, knowing that she didn't want help, but his hands were still reaching for the chair, a slight smile on his face as he watched her emotions flickering across hers.

"Brandon? That folder? What happened to it?" Hagen stopped him at the desk.

"Barnabas has it. He said all the guys have a copy and once they have done all they can on their own, they'll compile it. He said it should be in the next day or so." He perched on the edge of the desk, hands resting on his thigh, staring past her.

"I see. Did I really do that?"

"You did." He brought his gaze back to her. "I gave him another name." He paused, not quite sure how to continue.

"Ben." At his surprised look and nod, she drew in a deep breath. "I never felt comfortable around him. To put it mildly, he was too inquisitive, wanting to know things that were none of his business. Mom always avoided him." She looked up, a mixture of emotions still running across her face. "How do you continue to work for him?"

"I talked to Barnabas and resigned from there. I think I have been remiss. We have not discussed how us guys are paid. The Foundation pays us directly, letting our employers hire more personnel as they need to without worrying about finances. And since we married, you have a salary settled on you."

"I do? Why? I don't need it. At least, I don't think I will." Hagen was surprised.

"It's how the Foundation set it up. When we marry, our wives automatically become part of the Foundation family and then receive a salary as well. They can do what they want, work, volunteer, stay at home, go to school. And as with Darby, Haley and Holly will receive funding, particularly for their schooling. It's part of the Foundation mandate for being encouragers." He watched the tears pooling in her eyes before he was on his knees, carefully wrapping her in his arms. "I'm sorry. I shouldn't have told you like that."

Hagen finally just laid her head on his shoulder, exhaustion over taking her, her eyes slipping closed against the pain as well. Brandon simply gathered her up and carried her to the bedroom, carefully letting her lie down before he pulled a cover over her. He left and returned with the wheelchair, glad the rooms were not small. He stood for a moment before he stretched out beside her, carefully cradling her to him, and then slept as well.

———

Haley and Holly went looking for them when they returned, Blair walking them to their door, before he headed for the conference room. Something was puzzling him and he needed to work on that. He knew Devaney would come and find him at some point. He could use her ideas, he thought.

Holly paused in the doorway, a faint blush on her cheeks, her eyes on her sister before she looked at Brandon who had roused and pushed himself upright.

"Holly? School all done?" He rose, heading to hug her and then searching for Haley to do the same.

"It is. And we don't have to go next week. It's a holiday." Haley looked past him. "We would usually do something fun, but I guess we can't."

"We still might be able to. Let's see how Hagen is at the beginning of the week. Now, what have you to tell me about your day?"

The twins chattered away, answering his questions, and just giving details of their day, responding with laughter at his teasing.

Holly finally shared a look with Haley. "Brandon, I have to tell you something, only I don't know how to."

"Just talk. That's all you need to do." Brandon leaned back against the kitchen counter, drying his hands and then throwing the towel over one shoulder. He had heard the faint squeak of the wheelchair, and know Hagen was heading their way.

"It's about Ben. I don't trust him. He's been hanging around the school, trying to talk to us. We've avoided him as much as we can. Why?" Holly looked frightened for a moment.

"That's what we're working on. Our guys are searching. Dallas is as well. I know what you mean. That's why I don't work for him anymore." He looked between the girls, seeing their startled glances at him and then each other. "It's okay. We'll be okay. I am going to use this time to help your sister heal, help you two through the rest of the school year and then decide what I want to do."

"But Brandon? You can't quit. How do you live then?" Haley reached to hug Hagen, who had wheeled into the kitchen at that point and sat listening to her sisters, and then stood, an arm around her.

"It's fine, Haley. I'm paid by the Foundation, as is Hagen now that we're married. And you two will receive funding from them, particularly for your schooling." He watched as the surprise and then excitement filled their faces.

"You mean, Hagen doesn't have to strive to save so much? She can do what she really dreams of doing with her work?" Haley danced around the room, reaching for Holly and pulling her with her. "God is good."

"He is that and all the time. Now, listen, what you said about Ben? Stay away from him as much as you can."

"It's hard." Holly flopped down into a chair. "He seems to be wherever we are."

"I understand that. The guys know that, too. They want to escort you two lovely ladies as much as they can."

Chapter 28

A week later, Hagen approached her shop. She had not been able to bring herself to go there, but Brandon had been back and forth. He had grinned when she grumped at him for doing that.

"The guys and ladies are working in there. Darby is particularly interested, you know."

"He is? He's good with his hands. Maybe I need to hire him part-time, for now." She hesitated as Brandon pushed her chair through the door, her mind freezing as she remembered the assault. Looking around, her hands went out to stop the chair, a surprised and then delighted look on her face. "Brandon? What did they do?"

"Barnabas had it repainted and rearranged for you. The guys worked with him. I think I like this set up better."

Hagen nodded, seeing the wall that now stood between the work area and the lobby or reception area, noting as she wheeled through the door that there was a lock on it. Brandon caught her quick glimpse at it.

"Bradon insisted on that. Branigan has worked his magic with a security system for you. He had been planning on doing just that for you, but had wanted to talk to you first."

"I see." Hagen's thoughts were already on her workshop, wheeling her way around it, hands reaching out to touch and then withdraw. She sighed, still not quite comfortable. The attack had left her badly shaken and fearful.

"Hagen? What more can we do for you?" Brandon crouched down beside her, an arm around her.

"I don't know, Brandon. They have done so much." She looked up as the door opened and frowned. "Brandon, the door. Lock it please."

Brandon was on his feet, the door shut and quietly locked, watching the man who had entered. He had a bad feeling about him, his work in the social field giving him a sixth sense about people.

"Can we help you?" Brandon stood in front of the window, his eyes watchful, his hand reaching for the button just under the counter that Branigan had reinstalled when he was done his work.

"No, I am just looking around. I would like to come in there and see up close what there is."

Brandon shook his head. "Sorry. Not happening. It's all on a website that you can look at and order from. This is a private business."

"No need to be hostile. I'm interested in investing in this business. I hear the owner is looking for money to come in and help build it." The man, short, stocky, grizzled in appearance reached to try the door, surprised to find it locked.

Brandon heard Hagen's choked cry before he shook his head, his eyes going past the man to the security guards standing just inside the door.

———

"No, I don't think so. That's not why you're here. These gentlemen behind will escort you to the security office. We have a police officer on the way to speak with you." Brandon watched as the man jerked and then stepped backwards, surprise flittering across his face, an emotion that was quickly hidden.

"That's not necessary. Not at all. I'll come back." He made to move past the three guards, but was prevented by a hand on his arm. He was led away, protesting the whole time.

Hagen, who had stayed hidden, pushed herself forward, frustrated that she couldn't be on her feet. She was healing but the uncertainty as to if she would heal completely was still there. She paused beside Brandon, fear and anger on her face.

"Do you know who that was?"

Brandon shook his head. "No, I'm sorry. I don't." He was watching the door intently, not catching the look of frustration that showed momentarily on his bride's face.

"That was Ben's brother."

"Brother? I never knew he had a brother." Brandon finally looked down at her, puzzled.

"It's his half-brother. They always tried to pretend they didn't get along and didn't want anything to do with one another, but that's not the case." Hagen spun, reaching for the lock on the door, frustrated as she had trouble getting the door open, before she wheeled through, heading for the outside door, Brandon behind her, reaching to hold the door.

"Hagen?" He paused to set the alarm and then lock the door before he had to almost run after her. "Hagen?"

"I need to see your friends. To see which one is working on that name. Or are they?" She stopped suddenly, pain crossing her face for a moment. "I hate this, Brandon. I hate this chair. I hate that I'm restricted. How do I go on?" She shoved away from him, not waiting for an answer.

Brandon stood, shocked for a moment, his hands on the top of his head, not quite sure how to react. He knew Hagen was still hurting, and not just physically. He had tried to get her to talk to him, to talk to someone, but she had shut down and then wheeled away, heading for the balcony, struggling to open the door to get through, not willing to ask for help. Lord, how do I do this? How do I get her help? She has to be willing to seek it herself, but I am not sure she will, not unless something else happens. And, dear Lord, that scares me. I don't want to lose her, or one of the twins.

Brandon followed slowly, his hands jammed into his jeans pocket, feeling the coolness of the breeze blowing in from Lake Erie. He shivered, but not just from that. He stopped short, and then wandered around the building, intending to walk the paths before he sought Hagen once more. So engrossed was he in his thoughts that he didn't hear the running footsteps behind him, not until an arm snaked around his neck and a knife dug into his side. He was propelled forward before he could fight to free himself, a second man slapping a blindfold and gag roughly over his face before pulling his hands behind him and binding them with rough rope that scraped at his wrists. He was shoved into a waiting van which took off rapidly, the dust from its travel seeking the sky before it settled back down on the ground. He lay, his breath knocked from him with the force he had been slammed into the metal van floor, his head bouncing against the floor from the roughness of the ride as the van travelled rapidly over a gravel road, hitting ruts and potholes, finally with a hard enough force that he drifted off as he lost consciousness.

Chapter 29

Lost in thought and in her research, Hagen didn't notice the passing time. She vaguely heard the comings and goings around her, raising her head once when Holly and Haley had approached her before they took off on their own tangent. She finally slumped back in the chair, her hands rubbing at her face, fatigue drawing deep lines in her face while adding a grayish shine to it. There had to be something here, she thought. There just has to be.

The noise of a chair sliding back beside her had her jumping, a hand to her throat, as she looked that way. Brennen grinned at her, Brody on his other side, both of them watching her.

"You have been deep in that, whatever it is." Brennen pointed to the papers she was tidying together.

"I have been and for too long." She looked around. "Where is everyone?"

"Gone for their meal or off to other activities. Where's Brandon?" Brody looked around, not having seen him since Hagen had entered the conference room.

Hagen shrugged. "I thought he was in here. Didn't I hear him?" When both men shook their heads, she sighed. "He was in the shop with me with Ben's brother, Billy, entered. We were heading this way. I haven't seen him since." She didn't tell the men how ashamed she felt for how she had reacted.

"No, he hasn't been. We haven't seen him. The twins were asking if we had. He had said something about a hike tonight with them." Brennen and Brody exchanged a glance, not liking the feeling they were getting.

"They haven't?" Hagen paused, ready to push herself away from the table, when she reached for the paperwork. "I need one of you to look over. I have determined that both Ben Richards and his brother, Billy, are involved. Billy was the one who was in the shop today."

"Wait a minute!" Brody's hand was up, stopping her words. "What man? In your shop?"

She nodded. "Earlier, just before I came in. The security came and took him. Brandon may be looking into that, mightn't he?"

"He might." Brody was on his feet, striding rapidly away from the room, searching for the security guard, not liking that they had not seen Brandon either since the incident. Brody headed outside, looking for Bradon and his dog, Kade, knowing that more than likely, Brandon had disappeared once more. Now, he thought, just how do I tell Hagen that, Lord? Thanks, You just had to hand it to me.

Brennen watched him walk away before he turned back to Hagen. His eyes narrowed as he caught how exhausted and in pain she was. Reaching for the papers she held, he took them gently from her, setting them on the table.

"Right now, Hagen, we need to get you home. You've done too much." He stood, his hands on her chair to pull it back and then head for the door.

Hagen gave a weary nod, wanting nothing more than to find her bed and sleep. Thanking Brennen as he opened and then closed the door to the apartment behind her, she slowly wheeled through the place, looking for the girls or Brandon, and not seeing any of them. She sat for a moment, contemplating the shower before she turned away, shifting instead to her bed and laying down, reaching for a light blanket. She was asleep almost instantaneously, not hearing the outside door fly open and the girls run through it, looking for either one of them.

The twins stood in her bedroom door, their eyes on her, before looking at each other. They had not found Brandon, no matter where they had looked. His truck was still there, so where was he?

"We can't wake her, Holly." Haley shifted from foot to foot. "We just can't. But, where is Brandon?"

"That we need to find out." Holly's phone was out, as she dialled his number once more, with it going straight to voice mail. "He's not answering. Where is he?"

"I know. Holly, I'm so worried. What if he's disappeared?"

Holly spun, anger briefly on her face. "He can't, Haley. He just can't. Hagen needs him too much." She ran as she heard a tap at the door, knowing it wouldn't be Brandon, but just praying it was someone who could tell them where he was.

———

Holly pulled the door open, Haley standing right behind her. a hand to her sister's back. They stared at Breck and Brennen, who stood there, trying to hide the grimness of their faces behind smiles but unable to do so.

"May we come in, ladies?" Breck pointed behind them. "We need to talk to Hagen."

"She's sleeping, Breck." Holly spoke as she backed away, not sure what to do or which room to go to.

"How about the kitchen, Holly?" Brennen headed that way, the ease of friendship with Brandon letting him do just that. "Have you eaten?"

The twins exchanged glances before Haley spoke. "No, we haven't."

"Sit. I'll make some sandwiches. Breck and I haven't eaten, and I'm starved." Brennen was desperate to lighten the mood, knowing that what they had to say would take the girls' appetites, unless they were fed first.

Rousing from her sleep, Hagen brushed at her long hair, finally braiding it and reaching for the tie around her wrist. She frowned, hearing men's voices from the other end of the apartment. Her head tilting, she listened before she shook it. No, that was not Brandon's voice. Who would be here?

Without thinking, she stood and walked towards the door, a muscle spasm in her back stopping her for a moment before she reached for the wall, her hand running along it as she walked towards the kitchen, pausing in the doorway, her eyes on the twins before they raised to the two men. Breck just shook his head at her, watching as she caught her breath in a half-sob and her face crumpling before she schooled her features and walked into the kitchen, Brennen pulling back a chair for her, his hand out to help her sit before it rested briefly on her shoulder.

Haley and Holly stared at her, but before they could ask her where her chair was, Breck sat beside Hagen, handing her a cup of tea, knowing that her preference had changed.

"How are you, Hagen?" Breck's voice was low, almost as if he were afraid to ask.

Hagen shrugged. "To tell you the truth, I really don't know how I'm to feel. Exhausted. Overwhelmed. Burdened. Saddened. Lost." She kept her eyes on Breck. "And losing my dreams. How does that sound?"

"Sounds about right to me." Breck had heard a sound from Haley, he thought it was. "Have you eaten?"

Hagen shook her head. "No, I went right to sleep. A sandwich sounds good." She went to push away from the table, looking up with a word of thanks as Brennen served her.

Breck finally bowed his head, bringing the ladies to God, and then praying for Brandon, knowing he had news he did not want to share with Hagen.

Hagen studied him as he raised his head, his eyes steady on her. She nodded.

"You have word? He's gone, isn't he?"

Chapter 30

Breck drew in his breath, still not used to the direct way that Hagen had of speaking.

"He is, Hagen. I'm sorry. We've searched. Bradon had Kade out and tracked him to the end of the forest." Breck's eyes met Brennen's. "I wish we could fence it off and stop this from ever happening again."

"It's happened before?" Holly's voice was barely audible as her hands reached for both Haley and Hagen.

"It has, Holly. In fact, Guenivere disappeared right out of her apartment. We have attempted to block any further attempt, but we can't lock up the outdoors, as much as we would like to."

Hagen's head dropped to her folded arms, a shudder running through her before her head raised again, determination on it.

"Do we know anything at all?"

Breck shook his head. "Dallas is out here now. They're searching. He'll want to talk to you about this afternoon."

"I thought he would. Will those two never leave us alone?" She grew pensive, not seeing the questions trembling on the twins' lips and faces. "Have they found Ben?"

"Not yet. And Billy wasn't arrested, for some reason, even though Barnabas pressed for just that."

"Who was the responding officer? Buddy Fuller?" At Breck's nod, she sighed once more, her eyes raised to the heavens as she prayed for peace, for strength, for courage, and for her anger to be removed. "That's Billy's son. He goes by his mother's name. I am sure that Barnabas would not have known that. If Will had, Buddy would not have been near here. We need to take out an order to keep him away from here and away from the twins and myself."

Breck was on his feet, excusing himself, angry that this had happened. His phone out, he spoke abruptly with Barnabas, who promised to talk to both Dallas and Will. He turned back, catching Hagen for a moment as she sat, the sadness that he could sense almost overwhelming. Breck was back in his chair, listening as Brennen and Hagen spoke.

"Where would they take him?" Hagen looked around, Haley on her feet and running to the office, to return with paper and pens and Hagen's laptop.

"Where do we start, Hagen?" Holly leaned over Haley's chair, watching as Haley's finger flew over the keyboard.

"Breck? Brennen? What would you suggest?"

"We start with here. Then, we move outwards. Bradon said it looked as if the vehicle had taken off rapidly, heading down the gravel road that runs towards the highway."

"There are a lot of places that they could pull off and hide along there. A number of old abandoned buildings. Houses where the people are away or up north for vacations for the summer. The ones where people have already closed up and headed south for the winter." Hagen chewed at her lip, her hand idly twisting her cup, before Brennen stood, reached to refill it, and then sat back down.

"We can start a search but we can't go on private property. That we would have to leave for the police."

"Couldn't you drive in and then back out?" Haley was puzzled. "I mean, what if it is a place where you know the people? Couldn't you go see if they were home?"

"We could, Haley, but we have to be so careful. We can't compromise the investigation."

"And that might do it. I get it." Haley sat back, blowing out a breath that stirred her bangs. She began to pull at them before she reached for the laptop again, whispering to Holly, who nodded and watched as Haley pulled up a topographical map program.

Breck rose, to move his chair closer to the twins, watchful as he studied what they were doing.

"What are you planning to do with that? What's your purpose?"

Holly frowned at him. "You sound like one of our teachers." Her comment brought grins to the men's faces for a moment. "We want to see what the land looks like, if there are a lot of buildings, or if there is any provincially or federally owned land. We wouldn't need permission to walk on it, would we?"

"It depends, Holly, what the land is. Around here, I don't remember hearing of any that we couldn't do that with. I can check with a friend to make sure."

Hagen looked around. "I know who we can talk to. A friend of Dad's that used to work in the county. He can help." She stopped, biting at her lip. "No, I guess we can't. He's related to Ben and Billy."

"And he would be the perfect one to help them set up a hiding place, now wouldn't he?" Brennen bit out his words, anger lacing them. "Let me have his name, Hagen. He's just gone on our list."

Hagen supplied it, not seeing the surprise that flickered across the men's faces. They knew the name. He had been prominent in their church at one point until differences on the board had sent him away to another church, where they heard that he was causing similar problems.

Hagen turned as she heard her phone. "My phone? Where did I leave it now?"

Haley was on her feet, running for the bedroom and back, handing it to her sister. "I don't know that number, Hagen. Do you?"

Hagen nodded, swiping across her phone to answer it. "Elizabeth? Hi. How are you? Me? I'm hurting, but why are you calling?" Hagen gave a low laugh. "You heard what? Yes, I am. And yes, Abe and Emma have met him. So, he's approved." She listened for a few moments, her head nodding every once in a while, before she reached for a pen and paper. "What did Emma say? Is that right? Who? Yes, we have his name. I know. I wasn't to have an adventure like you and Nathaniel, now was I? You set an example for me, all of you." She laughed before she drew in a breath. "How much does she have? I see. And who is bringing it? Oh, wonderful. I would love to see you and Nathaniel. Who else? Good. The twins? They're good." Hagen paused, her eyes on her sisters. "Elizabeth? You've mentioned you heard I was having problems. It's Brandon. He went missing today." Hagen's finger moved around the table, Hagen not really knowing what she was doing, the twins' gazes tight on her. "Thank you, my friend. I do appreciate that. Tomorrow? I think so. I mean, I'll be here. Since I was hurt, I haven't been travelling. Hurt? We'll talk. And thank you. And thank Emma. What was that? Do I need all of you? Like in how many?" Hagen laughed once more before she clicked off from her call and then set her phone carefully on the table, tears near the surface that she just could not hold back. The twins surrounded her, their tears mingling for a moment.

Chapter 31

A week later, Hagen walked slowly towards her shop, her interest in it greatly diminished. Where are you, Brandon? I miss you, my love. I want you with me. Lord, please? My heart can't take losing someone else I love.

She stopped short as she stared at the door, before she walked forward to reach for the envelope that was tacked to it. Her hands shook as she opened in and dumped out photos and a piece of paper. They fluttered to the ground as she stood, her eyes on them, not comprehending for a moment what they were. Dropping to her knees, her fingers moved among them, looking with horror at the pictures of Brandon, each one with a consecutive date on them, up until that very morning. Hagen reached for the note, her hands shaking violently as she did so, unable to stop the paper from shaking so that she could read it.

Blair and Benen had been heading for the gym and stopped short as they caught sight of her before running towards her, dropping beside her, Benen's eyes on Hagen, Blair's on the photos. Blair reached to gather them, shock on his face, before he turned to Benen.

"Inside with her, Benen. To the building."

Benen's arm around her raised Hagen to her feet, her hand still clutching the paper. She was rushed inside and then set gently into a chair, the others in the room looking up in surprise and then with grim visages as they were told what had been found.

Dallas appeared an hour later, his eyes studying Hagen before he turned to Benen and Blair.

"What do you have?" He watched the anger simmering in them.

"This!" Benen shoved the photos and letter at Dallas, who barely caught them. "Hagen found these. On the door to her shop. All on her own. No one was with her. We found her on her knees, frozen and shaking so badly we couldn't get her to stand on her own."

Dallas shifted so he could watch Hagen, seeing her wrapped in a blanket, a cup of tea in front of her that he doubted she had touched. He looked down then at the photos, dropping them to the table to sort through them, a pen in his hand to do so.

"I know you've touched them, but who all?"

"Hagen. Blair. Myself. The others know what they contain but have not seen them or handled them."

"Good. We can eliminate your prints and Hagen's then." Dallas turned his attention then to the note. "Did she read this?"

"We think so, but we're not sure. She was shaking so badly when we found her that the paper was moving almost too fast to even catch a glimpse of what was on it. I am not even sure if she had read it. She hasn't responded to us at all."

Dallas nodded, having seen behaviour similar to this before. "Has Doc been around?"

"He was on duty but is heading here shortly. Brady took a look at her before he left. He said just to watch her and if she didn't respond, then to take her in. So far, we haven't felt we have had to." Blair was frustrated. "This is enough already."

"It is." Dallas' eyes dropped to the note. "Did you read this?"

"Blair and I did." Benen stared down at it as well. "It's brutal, Dallas. No young lady should be told that the only way she'll see her groom of a few weeks is in his casket. What do they want from her?"

"Her business. Word on the street that we have verified is that they want to use it for smuggled drugs and jewels. Something similar to what they wanted with Guenivere's father's business." Dallas looked up, a frown on his face. "Are these related?"

"No, they're not." The three men turned to find Hagen standing there, haggard as to appearance, still fairly shaky. "The Richards brothers have always been near the line. Billy has been over more times that you can count. Dad was getting ready to have him charged." Her voice died away. "That's why. It's revenge, blackmail, what have you. Who else are they after?" Tears clogged her throat for a moment. "Where is Brandon? Can anyone tell me that?"

Hagen stared at them for a moment before she turned and ran from the room, a hand to her lower back, and disappeared up the stairs, hitting the door of the apartment with her hands and twisting at the knob to open it, before she continued to run towards the bedroom, throwing herself facedown on the bed, to sob heartbrokenly, only too glad that the girls were away with some of the ladies in the building.

Haley and Holly approached her later that afternoon, finding her cuddled down in her favourite chair on the balcony, a blanket wrapped around her once more. She didn't look up as they approached, leaving them to stare at one another before they sank to the floor, their eyes on her once more.

"Hagen? What happened?" Haley was almost afraid to ask.

"I received photos of Brandon and a ransom note. No, I won't tell you what was in it. I can't. Dallas has everything."

"Is he okay?" Holly spoke up, her eyes on Haley, who shrugged.

"No, he's not, girls. He's not. And I don't know where he is. How do we find him?"

Chapter 32

Losing track of the hours and days, Brandon paced his jail cell and that was exactly what it was. Whoever had abducted him had set up a mock cell, iron bars, rough bed, minimal facilities, just for him, he thought. He continued to pace, spending hours doing so, interspersed with standing at the small barred window, staring out into the day or night, whichever time of day found him there. He had become accustomed to the critters and insects that shared his cell, leaving crumbs for them.

Brandon despaired of getting loose. He had awakened finally two days after he had been abducted, his head pounding with pain. Being given nothing for the pain, he had suffered for days with a residual headache, just the last couple of days not being tormented by it. He was tormented with thoughts of Hagen and how she was and what this was doing to her. He knew they had taken pictures of him, they had forced him into a chair, to hold a paper he wasn't allowed to read, before he was shoved back into his cell.

Ben Richards stood and watched him through the bars, waiting for Brandon to turn. When he didn't, the anger began to burn within him.

"Brandon? Turn around." Ben's voice was harsh, not something Brandon had heard from him before.

Brandon refused to move, his eyes focused on the birds whirling in the sky, wishing he was as free as they were. He ignored his former employer, realizing for the first time that he had not really known him and wondered just how he had made it through the stiff interview and investigative process the Foundation put their prospective employers through. He was sure Barnabas would be looking into that with a fine tooth comb.

Ben began to yell at Brandon, his hands grasping at the bars, spittle flying from his mouth in his rage. It was a good thing, Brandon thought, that the door is locked and he doesn't have the key to it. He felt at his neck, feeling where Ben's hands would have been on them if they could have been.

Ben finally turned, a final taunt thrown over his shoulder, that Hagen would never find him and that Ben would claim her for his own. Brandon spun at that, horror on his face as he rushed towards the bars, reaching through in a desperate attempt to stop him. He sagged against the bars, unable to reach him to stop him, his mind racing as to how he could do that.

Brandon sank to the floor, his head bent to touch it, his arms wrapping around his head, sorrow and fear shaking him to the core. His heart cried out to God, but he just couldn't put into words his thoughts. Protect her, was all he could manage.

Two days later, he looked up, a frown on his face, from where he sat on the edge of his bed. Billy Richards stood there, an impassive look on his face, his eyes not moving from watching Brandon.

Brandon waited, not speaking, just waiting, he thought, for what, he had no idea. He refused to look away, refused to back away, refused to speak.

"Not talking?" Billy gave a sneer. "Ben said you would talk, that you couldn't help yourself."

Brandon didn't respond to the taunts hurled at him. He couldn't. He wouldn't do anything that would hurt the love of his life.

Billy finally stepped back from the bars, turning to speak to someone, a voice that had Brandon frowning before he covered it with an impassive face. He knew that voice and it was someone high up in the town council, someone he had had dealings with on multiple occasions. Why was she here?

Billy turned back to him, anger on his face. "Do you know my brother has been arrested? And that he has assaulted in jail? This is your fault. You will never leave here, not as long as you live, and I can guarantee you that won't be long." Billy spun on his heel and stormed away, his feet hitting hard on the stone floor.

Brandon sank back on the bunk, his head hitting the thin pillow, before his eyes closed. Lord, I can't do this. I can't live like this. It will kill me. That I know. I just want to be free, to be with Hagen, to help her reach her dreams, and just maybe have a few dreams of our own come true. He finally slept, exhaustion hitting him hard. He didn't see the man who appeared, looking over his shoulder, before he reached to unlock the cell and creep on silent fee towards Brandon.

A hand reached out to shake Brandon with no effect. The man shook his head at that, before he reached to draw Brandon to his feet and then over his shoulder, the cell door closed and locked behind him. The man, young but somewhat older than Brandon, a beard covering his lower face, a pulled down cap covering the rest, headed for the corn field behind the house, maneuvering his way through the cornstalks until he reached another road, where an old truck waited. He dropped Brandon to the passenger seat and buckled his seatbelt before carefully and quietly closing the door, his hand resting for a moment on the window as he looked around. He crept around to his own door, closing it quietly behind him as well, before he keyed the well-tuned motor to life, pulling away and heading towards the Foundation building and then past it, to arrive at a small working farm where he pulled through the open door in the drive shed, stopping the truck, pulling the key from the ignition and then running to close the doors after a careful look around.

Brandon stirred briefly as his door was opened and his eyes flickered open before he slept again, the nights of little or broken sleep and the strain and stress that he had been under with Hagen's injury combined to drive him back down in the depths of sleep and unconsciousness. The man shook his head before pulling Brandon from the truck, driving a shoulder into his abdomen and carefully situating him over his shoulder. He turned, heading for the loft in the drive shed where a soft clean bed waited for Brandon.

Brandon sighed as he sank down, murmuring a quiet thank you, not feeling his boots being pulled from his feet and then the socks that he had worn for so long. The man stood over him before he headed for the small bathroom attached, wringing out a cloth in warm water and soap and returned to wash Brandon's face and hands and then his feet.

He stood back, eyes on the far wall before he turned and headed back out the door, closing it quietly before he walked down the steps, his boot heels sounding hollow on them. He. stood, his eyes on the loft before he shook his head and walked away, closing the side door to the building after himself. Brandon would sleep, he thought, for a while, at least until he was able to find some food for him.

Chapter 33

Her head hurting from lack of sleep, Hagen paced her workshop. She was alone, the door to the reception area locked. She should be working, but she had no interest in it. Her heart cried hourly to God, asking for Brandon to come home, so that they could go on with the dreams that they had been starting to talk about.

She turned to her work, picking up a puzzle and staring at it, her mind working overtime for a moment in what she wanted to do. She dropped the puzzle, reaching instead for a pad of paper and a pen, ideas flowing from her with detailed description as to colour, size, material, age group. Hagen finally sat back, drained, not sure why she felt she had to put down all her ideas. She was on her feet, finding samples for each plan, each plan going into its own folder, her ideas transferred to her design program and copies printed.

Hagen finally sat back, drained, unsure why still but knowing that was what God had wanted. She reached for her water bottle, taking a deep swig, as she heard the outside door open. She stepped to where she could see who had come in, a surprised look on her face.

"Daniel? What are you doing here? I thought you were deep in farm work at this time of day." She reached to unlock the door, heading through it to stand in front of an old friend, Daniel Fields.

"I should be, Hagen, but I had to see you. Can we talk in here without being overheard?"

She nodded. "We can. Everyone is away or busy. The twins are at school."

Daniel rubbed his hands down his jeans, not sure how to start. He stared at the young lady in front of him, knowing that what he had to tell her would rock her world and set her on a mission, but he had to be sure first that she would be safe

"Daniel?" Hagen stared at him. "You usually don't have any trouble talking to me."

He gave a small grin, before sobering. "I know, Hagen. I know. But this time, it's hard. It involves more than just you and me." He spun to pace, his hand running through the blond hair he kept cropped short. He spun back, to come to stand in front of her. "Hagen, is it true? You're married?"

Hagen nodded, her smile sad. "I am, Daniel. Only he was kidnapped by someone trying to take over my business."

"It's growing? I have heard good things about it. He's from here, isn't he?"

"He is. I think you've met him at church. Brandon.'

"I have." Daniel looked down for a moment at the fingers he was rubbing together. "Hagen. I need you to do something for me. I need you to pack a bag for yourself and for Brandon."

Hagen stared at him. "A bag? For both of us?" At his nod, she frowned before her face lit up. "You know where he is? Where?"

Daniel shook his head. "Not yet. Go, do what I asked. I'll meet you at the rose garden. Try and keep it less than obvious what you're doing."

"I can try." She turned before she spoke. "The twins?"

"Ask Anna and Doc to look after them for you. Tell Doc I need to talk with him too."

Hagen turned back to stare at him before she turned and almost ran for the building, slipping up the back stairs to the apartment. She quickly grabbed clothes for both of them, hesitating for a moment before she called Anna.

"Anna? Can the twins stay with you and Doc? I have been called away to help a friend. That's great. Also, can you have Doc call Daniel Fields? That's right. Daniel. I ran into him today and he asked for Doc to call, that he had to talk to him. Okay. No, I'm not sure when I'll be home. I'll leave a paper authorizing you and Doc to look after them for now."

Hagen raced for the office, moving as quickly as she could, scribbling out a note for Doc and Anna and sealing it into an envelope before she left one for the twins.

"Haley and Holly: I've been called away for a few days. I'm okay. I am with a friend to help another friend. Doc and Anna will look after you. I'll try and call in a day or so, but I can't make any promises. Pray, dears, please pray. Help where you can in the research.

"I have left a whole whack of plans and whatnot in the shop. If you and Darby want, you can work on them, or whoever else wants to. I think we're caught up, just needing to do some new stuff. Love you.

"Hagen."

Hagen dropped the note on the kitchen table, beside the envelope for Anna, where she knew the twins would find it. She grabbed the charger cords for the phones, dropping them into a pocket, and then ran for the door, ignoring the twinges of pain that coursed through her at times.

Daniel was waiting for her near the perennial garden, motioning for her to be quiet and then heading away from the building, taking a path that Hagen didn't recognize, that came out near a paved lane. Daniel held the truck door for Hagen and then ran for his own seat, heading away as quickly as he could.

"Daniel?" Hagen waited until he glanced at her. "Brandon?"

"I have Brandon, Hagen. He's in my drive shed, in the loft you helped me design for whoever needed it. I never expected it would be you."

"Your drive shed? But how?"

"I'll explain. Just let me get you to him. I think he's beginning to give up, Hagen. I found him locked in a cell, one I think that was designed just for him."

"Ben and Billy Richards."

Daniel shot her a startled glance, his face not able to hide his surprise. "I think so, but there's someone else involved."

"I know. A woman. Only a woman would or could be this vindictive. And I think I know who."

"If you do, have you told anyone?"

Hagen shook her head. "No. I need to but I don't know which of the guys to tell."

"Who do you know the best?"

"Brady." She sighed. "He's married to Fynn, right, and Alice is married to Fynn's brother, Farr."

"Then, that's who you'll tell. Wait for a bit, just until you find Brandon."

Chapter 34

Reaching for her duffle bag, Daniel merely pointed to the stairs to the loft, before he headed to roll down the door, and then followed Hagen as she slowly made her way to the landing. He reached past her to open the door, setting the bag inside, and then reached to hug her, a prayer whispered in her ear. He watched as she hesitated, a hand to her mouth, tears sparkling in her eyes before she stepped through into the living room, not even acknowledging the door closing being her.

Daniel stood, his head back against the door, his eyes closing for a moment as emotions roiled within him. Hagen had been his best friend growing up, a sister to him. He hated to see what was happening to her. He finally moved away, heading for his fields, to see what he could accomplish, but his mind puzzled through what Hagen and Brandon were facing.

Moving quietly towards the bedroom, Hagen hesitated for a moment before she touched the door with her fingertips, her other hand across her mouth to still her sobs. She stood for a moment in the half-light, searching for Brandon, finally seeing him on his side on the bed, an arm wrapped around his chest, the other wrapped around his head. She gave a half-cry before she fled towards him, dropping to her knees, arms trying to surround him, unable to lift his weight to do just that. Her head was buried against him as sobs shook her body.

Thank you, Lord. He's out. He's safe. Now, please, Lord, help us to solve this, to find out who it is. I can't live like I did. It's not fair to the twins, either.

Brandon stirred, his arm coming from around his head, a hand dropping on her head before he slept once more, relief that he didn't realize he was feeling coursing through him. Hagen finally raised her head, her eyes on his face, a hand reaching to touch him, unable to fully comprehend that he was here and that she was with him. She finally rose, reaching for the blanket draped across the footboard, shaking it out to cover him, and then heading to find a hot damp washcloth to wash her face. Her tears had been cathartic, much needed. Hagen stood at the window in the living room, seeing the darkening of the evening, and knowing she would need to find Daniel.

Daniel turned as he heard her footsteps approaching him where he stood contemplating his house garden. He needed to get into it, he had been thinking, and pick what was ripe, and that was a lot.

"Hagen?"

"Thank you, Daniel. I don't know how you knew where he was or that he was even missing. Or that he belonged to me or me to him. He's sleeping more soundly now, not as restlessly." Hagen wrapped her arms around herself against the chill of the evening. "What can you tell me?"

"The old Richards place? He was there but hidden." Daniel felt his anger growing. "They had built a jail cell for him, and that's where he was. I happened to overhear Billy talking on the phone this morning. You know how loud he can talk and how most times he really doesn't care if he's overheard. I had to search for the room. It was in the old barn, at the back of it. If you hadn't been looking for it, you would never have found it. Why go to all that work?"

"Simple. They want my business. Billy had someone assault me. I hadn't connected them until Billy showed up in the shop one day. I was told they were taking over my business and would use it for transporting drugs and stolen jewels."

"That's what we always expected from them, but no one has ever been able to prove it. How did Brandon end up working for them?"

"Ben hid his true character. Brandon was hired to work as a social worker for him, being paid by the Foundation. Greed took over, I think. Dad suspected something and I think was getting ready to go to the authorities." Hagen paled. "There's a safe in the office at the house. I haven't had the heart to open it." She looked at Daniel, horrified. "What if there's proof there, that I could have brought out? And prevented this from happening?"

"I don't know that it would have made a difference. Can I get it for you?"

Hagen nodded. "I'll get the keys and the combination in the morning." She turned slightly, looking back towards the drive shed. "We need to let the Foundation guys know." She signed as her phone rang and she pulled it out, reaching to mute it. "It's Brady. Now, what?"

"Answer it. You have to talk to one of them. Brady knows you. Or else talk to Barnabas. He'll need to know where Brandon is, but I'm not sure that is such a good idea."

She shrugged. "I have no idea." She finally swiped to answer the phone, Brady just kept calling her.

"Hagen? Where are you?" Brady's voice held a quality that she didn't think she had heard before.

"With friends. Why? I talked to Anna."

"We know you did. Elizabeth was here, looking for you. Emma sent more material. We need to discuss it."

"I can't, Brady. I'm in the midst of something right now." She was desperate not to give away anything but she couldn't be sure that she wouldn't.

"At least, Hagen, let me call you in the morning and do a conference call with some of the guys. They're worried, Hagen. I don't think you understand that you're part of our family now."

"I know I am, Brady. It's just so hard." She blinked rapidly, and then was running across the lawn, her phone tossed towards Daniel, who caught it and then swiped it to end her call, Brandon's name on her lips.

Brandon slowed to a stop, unable to believe what he saw. He just opened his arms and caught his bride, wrapping her tight to him, their tears mingling.

———

171

Daniel stood, watching for a moment, before he turned and walked towards his house, setting Hagen's phone on the table on the porch.

Chapter 35

Staring at his phone, Brady shook his head. Hagen was hiding something, that much he knew. He looked up, to see the other twelve men staring at him. He shrugged.

"She won't say where she is." He was apologetic.

"That doesn't surprise me. She doesn't know us well enough, I think." Brendon paused, a frown on his face. "You don't suppose...?" His voice died away, as he stared at Brady.

Brady nodded. "I think your supposition is likely correct. She's somehow found Brandon, and doesn't want to give away where they are."

"Would she do that?" Blair lifted his mug to sip from it, grimacing at the cold taste, before he rose, dumped it out and fixed himself a fresh mug, sitting back where he had been.

"I can see that." Barnabas spoke. "We have to let her do what she feels is best. If we push, she may grow stubborn on us." He looked around as the door opened, and Doc walked through, a tired look on his face. "Doc?"

Doc sat, scrubbing at his face with both hands, before rubbing at the back of his neck.

"Barnabas, what I am about to say, goes not further. It is third-hand knowledge." He looked around at the men, knowing that they would not break confidence with him. "I talked to Daniel Fields a bit ago."

"Daniel? What has he to do with this?" Buckley spoke for the group before he nodded. "The loft."

Doc nodded. "Daniel wouldn't say, but that's what I suspect. He said in a roundabout way that he had a friend who had been hurt in some manner, and that he had connected that friend with another friend."

Burnie snorted, causing the other men to smile. "He couldn't come right out and say, now could he? He has Hagen and Brandon with him, they're safe in his loft, and what do we want to do about it? That sound about right?"

Breck began to laugh. "Burnie, I think you need to go write something. You're beginning to talk in riddles."

Burnie grinned. "But I'm right, am I not?"

Brady nodded. "I think so. Doc, did Daniel say anything else?"

"He did. In a rambling manner, totally unlike him, he mentioned Ben and Billy Richards but also a woman. Carol Richards Balsam."

"Their sister?" Blair sat back. "Of course. She works for customs. That's the inside person we were trying to find." He sat forward, reaching for a pen and paper. "Now, we'll get somewhere, won't we?"

"Where's that stuff Elizabeth dropped off?" Bradon was on his feet, reaching for it and then sorting it out, handing some off to Brennen and Benen. "Here. It's going to be a long night, I suspect."

"I suspect you're right. Carol Richards has at least two other names. She's been married, what two or three times?" Baird spoke up.

"Try four. We know her by her last marriage. Unless you know her history, you wouldn't know that and therefore, wouldn't connect her to her brothers. They avoid each other." Breck turned to his laptop, beginning to search, not liking what he was finding in just a cursory one. "She's a nasty bit of work."

"What about properties? Do we have a list of those?" Baird reached for some of the paperwork.

"No, I don't think we do." Buckley paused, a thought crossing his mind. "Now, if memory serves me correctly, there is an old abandoned farm of theirs, not too far from here."

"Perfect. We'll look into that. Do you have the address?" Brody's hand was out, waiting for Buckley to drop the slip of paper into it. "Has anyone heard from Emma?"

"I did." Branigan spoke up. "She said she has material she will either courier to us in the morning or send with someone. I suspect that someone to be Elizabeth and Nathaniel."

"Or Emma herself with Abe." Baird's voice held a note of amusement before his face sobered. "I don't like this, fellows. There are more than just the three siblings. Did anyone know that?"

Doc nodded, from where he had sat himself into a corner, watching the men at work. "There are five that are living. A brother and a sister were killed in a house fire when they were young. It was always thought to be arson."

Chapter 36

His legs stretched out in front of him, Brandon lounged in one of the green wicker chairs on Daniel's back porch in the early morning of the next day, a Bible open on his knee, a mug of coffee, his third already that day, on the small glass table beside him. He tilted his head to listen to the calls of the awakening birds and insects and other creatures, and the softening sounds of the night creatures seeking their rest. He tilted his head even further to watch a cricket meandering across the floor, stopping every few feet to sing. He was content, he thought, for the moment, here with Hagen. Brandon was worried about the twins, knowing that he had disappointed them that night, even though he could not prevent it.

Hagen watched from the large kitchen window over the farmhouse sink she was working at, helping Daniel prepare their breakfast, quiet conversation of long-time friends between them.

"Daniel? Are you in the fields today?"

"Today? It's Saturday, right? I have to check them out but I don't think there's much to do. It's getting late in the year and I only have the soybeans and corn to harvest. The corn will be done next week. Why?" He turned from the stove, spatula in hand from turning the frying ham and French toast. "Was there something you needed?"

"There is." Hagen pointed with a soapy finger. "I left my keys and the safe combination there. If you could retrieve whatever is in it." Her brow wrinkled as she tried to think of what all would be in there. "Just dump it into a bag and bring it here. But, please be careful. The back door would work best."

"The twins won't be around?"

Hagen shrugged. "I highly doubt it. They haven't been there much since we moved to the Foundation building. I think they've cleared out everything." She sighed, her eyes resting back on Brandon, watching as his head bent once more over the Book he held. "I need to talk to Brandon. I'm not sure the twins will want to keep the house, but I think we should likely sell it. There are too many memories there for me. Besides, we're content where we are."

"No rush for that." Daniel reached for some plates, dishing up their meal, and then pointing to the door. "If you would, I think everything is out there."

"Just the coffee and my tea. Here, let me." She reached to open the door, the sound startling Brandon and causing him to jump, a white look crossing his face.

"Brandon?"

"I'm okay." He stood, reaching for a plate and then a new mug of coffee she handed him.

Hagen finally stood, clearing away their meal, before she sat back down, a pad of paper in front of her, twisting a pen in her fingers.

"Brandon, we need to talk to Dallas today, but how do we do that? We have to have him take your statement."

"I know." Brandon sighed. "I just wish that we didn't have to." He rubbed at a wrist, unaware of what he was doing. "I don't want to go around them. I saw what has happened before. They get attacked and hurt. And with their ladies involved now, I don't what anything to harm them."

"We get that, Brandon." Daniel sat back, before he rose. "I'm heading in to get what you asked for, Hagen. Anything else?"

Hagen shook her head. "I don't think so. I want this to end, Daniel, and maybe what you retrieve from the safe will do that." Her eyes rested on Brandon, seeing he was not listening to their conversation. "You're friends with Dallas. Can you ask him to come out this morning, if possible? Find some ruse to do that?"

"I can." Daniel suddenly grinned. "I've been promising him produce. There's a lot that needs picked. He can come help himself today." He turned and walked away, his face sobering, his eye thoughtful. Lord, I have no idea how we do this. Someone is going to get hurt. I pray it isn't Hagen again, but I know it will be. Protect her and Brandon right now, Lord. I want to see her live to fulfill the dreams she has had and that she and Brandon have now.

Brandon watched Hagen turning her phone over and over. "It won't bite."

"I know." She sighed, her eyes on her rings before she spoke. "I was talking with Brady last night. He wants a conference call this morning. How do we do this, Brandon? It's not safe for you to reappear, at least not yet. You have to give your statement to Dallas." She jerked as she heard a car, ready to run for shelter, before she sat back. "And there's Dallas."

Dallas stood at the bottom of the few steps, his eyes on Brandon, before he spoke. "Hagen?"

Hagen sank back down, her hand reaching for Brandon's. "Dallas? You're here? Did Daniel call you?"

"No, actually, he didn't. I heard that Daniel had been in touch with Doc, and surmised I might find you there. You're not hiding very well from your family, you know." He walked up the steps, past them into the kitchen, and returned a few minutes later, a plate with a warmed up breakfast on it and a mug of coffee. He sat, his head bowed for a moment, before he began to eat, ignoring the couple, but with a sparkle of mischief in his eyes.

Finally, Dallas sat back, pushing away his plate and rested his elbows on the table, his eyes on Brandon. He knew Hagen was watching him closely, and he bit back his smile. It's okay, Hagen. I won't tell where you are. I come out to see Daniel every two to three weeks. People know that, so they won't think this strange. And where you are sitting, you're sheltered by the blinds that Daniel or you drew down this morning. And they know you and Daniel are friends, so they wouldn't think anything of you being here. Except if they thought you knew where Brandon was, and then they would be looking for you.

"Brandon? Can you talk to me? Tell me what transpired?" Dallas drew out his notepad and pen, his eyes searching Brandon's face.

"I don't know how much I can tell you. I remember being taken from the building, blindfolded, gagged, bound and then thrown into a van. A very bump ride, I must say. One of the deep ruts caused me to bang my head extremely hard and I don't remember anything until I woke up in a jail cell. There was a row of bars and then a barred window. Very primitive. Billy Richards would show up every little asking, making demands that made no sense. The last day, I remember hearing a woman's voice, but I don't know who that was. They were arguing, I think, their voices raised but I couldn't hear well through the solid wood wall that stood about five feet away from the bars. The last thing I remember was laying down and falling asleep. That is until last night when I walked out from that building over there and saw Hagen running towards me. I can't tell you much more. I was on my own. Billy would bring in my food once a day and then leave."

Dallas nodded. "It is about what I expected. Here, let me have a moment to transcribe into my program and then I'll print it for you to sign. Once I've done that, we'll talk about other things."

Hagen looked down at her phone she had her hand on. "It's Brady, Brandon. He wants to do a conference call. What do we do?"

Brandon reached to kiss her, before laying an arm around her shoulders. "Now that Dallas has my statement, we need to talk to him and the others. They're too good of friends to me for me to hide more than I am."

Hagen searched his face before she nodded, reaching for her phone, putting it on speaker after she had dialled Brady's number.

"Brady? Good morning."

"Hagen? You're okay? Can you talk to the twins for a moment?"

"Hagen? Where are you?" Haley's worried voice sounded across the air waves.

"I'm at a friend's, and no, I won't tell you. It's not safe. I'm in hiding. How are you two?"

"We're okay. Just miss you." Holly's voice sounded choked with tears. "Hagen, when are you coming home?"

"Soon, I hope and pray, Holly. Now, what are you two up to?" Hagen spoke to her sisters for a few moments, her eyes never leaving Brandon's face. "Okay, is Brady still there?"

"He is. Love you, Hagen."

"Hagen? Are you really okay?" Brady sounded worried.

"Are the twins gone? If they are, who all is with you?"

"All the guys are, Hagen, as well as Will. The twins are gone." Brady waited for a moment. "Hagen? What are you up to?"

"It's not Hagen that's up to something, Brady. It's me. Someone freed me, but I don't want to come home, not just yet. We need to go over some things and find out some more information." Brandon's voice left silence on the other side of the call.

Chapter 37

Shock on his face, Brady stared at his phone before looking around, seeing similar looks on everyone else's face but Buckley, and that was no surprise, he thought.

"Brandon. You're free. What can you tell us?" Barnabas spoke up.

"Not a lot. I was told I was held in the Richards old barn. They had done up a real-life cell for me. I was released by a friend, brought to his place, and that's where Hagen and I are right now. We don't want to come around until we can talk about how we do it. It was Billy Richards. He kept coming in, ordering me to tell Hagen she had to let him in as a silent partner, that they were taking over her business."

"We figured that one out." Bradon spoke up. "Who else?"

"I heard a woman's voice that last day."

"His sister. She's involved all the way. We're finding out stuff that we'll pass on to Dallas." Burnie heard a snicker from Brandon. "Brandon? Did I say something funny?"

"Considering that Dallas is sitting here with us, not really." Dallas snickered, bringing a grin to Brandon's face for a moment. "Now, what?"

"Now, what?" Barnabas spoke again. "What else can you tell me?"

"Not a lot. I only saw Billy and that briefly. He never stayed more than five or ten minutes. I saw no one else. I can't even tell you who abducted me, he nabbed me from behind."

"Your height?"

Brandon paused, not having thought of that. "I would say so, or close. I can't describe either one."

"Okay." Breck took up the conversation. "We've been at work, as has Emma. Dallas, she is still shooting us information, where she's finding it I have no idea."

"Have a patrol pick it up. I'll look at it later. Right now, we need to come up with a way to get these two home safely and without being seen." Dallas rubbed a finger along his forehead. "I'm at a loss."

"We could do what we did before, vehicle into the loading dock, and then up to the apartment. But with the twins here, that would be more difficult." Blair was thinking aloud.

"It would be. They wouldn't mean to say something, but they're teenagers. Something would slip it." Hagen knew her sisters and would defend them with her life, but she was also a realist, knowing that teenagers didn't always think before they spoke.

"We'll see what we can do, Brandon, Hagen. It's likely better if you are here and stay inside and stay put. Where you are now puts your friend in danger." Breck spoke, his voice slow as he pondered different scenarios.

"I know, Breck. I know that." Hagen was almost in tears, leading Brandon to slid his chair closer and wrap her in his arm, Dallas watching with a look of sympathy on his face. "Knowing Dallas, he probably wants to lock us up somewhere, and Brandon can't do that again."

"No, he can't." Dallas finally spoked. "Give me the highlights of what you have."

He wrote his notes rapidly, sometimes interrupting to clarify a fact, before he stared down at his pile of notes, and there was a pile. His pen tapped gently against his hand as he sank into deep thought.

"Benen? That comment you made about Carol. What was that again?"

"My comment? That I wondered if it was her or if it was her other sister. They are very similar in appearance and their voices are quite a bit alike. Carol has always seemed on the up and up. That Caren, that's a different story. From what I understand, she has always been one to take advantage of others, considering it due her. Would she be the one who was there?"

"I think it was, Benen. I know Carol's voice and it didn't quite sound like her. I thought it was the deflection through the door and my not being quite alert."

"I'll look at bringing her in for questioning. We seem to be tripping over her every time we turn around." Dallas shook his head at Hagen. "Hagen?"

Hagen sighed, her hands gripping together until her fingers turned white. "It has to be her. She and Dad locked horns many times, he had her in court over numerous issues. I could see this being revenge driven for her." She looked away. "And their other brother, Byron. He hasn't been around a lot lately, but I did see him in town a few weeks ago. In the rundown part of the Main Street."

"It was reported to the homeless shelter, Hagen. They've been watching for him for something else." Buckley's drifted through the phone to her. "I'm sure, if he's still there, he'll be turned in. He's done too many dirty tricks for them to let it go."

"I know he has. Their kids are the same." Hagen's voice stopped. "Have you looked into their families?"

"We're working on it. Dallas, Emma has been back in touch just now. She said Abe and the guys were heading this way for work and he would drop off a bundle of documents for you at the precinct. I just love the way she uses words." Burnie's happy beam could be heard loud and clear.

That broke the heaviness of the conversation as they all laughed, leaving a huge smirk on his face.

"Dallas, where do we stand with the investigation?" Brennen voiced the thought they had all been trying to avoid.

"Right now? Not where I want to be or would like to be. With these new names and with what I am sure Emma has sent on, I'll be working long hours on this and my other cases." He rose to his feet. "Listen, guys, I have to run. Keep in touch. Stay safe all of you. I have no doubt they would use any one of you to get to Hagen.”

With that sobering comment, Dallas walked away, leaving Brandon and Hagen staring at one another, as they were sure the others were.

“Listen, I have Daniel going in to my home to retrieve some stuff from a safe. I’m not sure what I’ll find, but I know there might be something.” Hagen bit at her lip, knowing she had placed her friend in danger. “I shouldn’t have done that. I placed him in danger, didn’t I?”

“Not necessarily. He’s been in and out of your house for years, Hagen.” Barnabas hastened to reassure her. “They would not like think anything of it, other than he had gone in for something he needed.”

“I hope so.” Hagen stared at Brandon, seeing the fatigue beginning to show. “Barnabas, how do we do this? How do we come home? I can’t hide from the girls, they need me too much.”

Brandon’s hand rested on her arm, as he leaned over, a kiss on her cheek. “Bring us home, Barnabas. Send someone out to Daniel’s and bring us home. Reroute him to the building.”

Chapter 38

Standing in the kitchen of their apartment, Hagen shuddered, her mind thinking how close it had been for Brandon. Thank you, Lord. You protected him and brought him back to me. Now, what, though, Lord? Where do we go from here? How do we find the ones responsible? We can't begin to go on with our dreams unless and until the Richards are caught. Will it take me going out there, putting myself on the line to bring them to justice?

She felt arms around her and she leaned back against Brandon, her own hands wrapping around his. Her head tilted to rest on his arm, she felt safe, loved, and secure, but not necessarily in that order.

"What are you thinking about so hard?" Brandon waited for her to respond, content just to hold her.

"I was wondering how we catch them. What if it means that I have to put myself out there?"

"If you do, we'll do everything to keep you safe. I can guarantee you that. The guys won't want anything to happen to you."

"I know that, Brandon, but there is always a danger. Did Breck say where they were in their investigation? I know they are looking, feeding stuff on to Dallas and Will."

"He didn't say." Brandon moved past her to fridge, an eye on the clock. "How be I grill something for supper?"

"Sound good." She heard the sound of the door opening and her eyes slid closed. "Are you ready for this?"

"No, but I don't think we have much choice." He grinned at her even as he sat the meat and vegetables he had pulled from the fridge on the counter. He turned, his grin becoming larger as he heard the bickering between the twins before they appeared in the kitchen doorway, their eyes on him before finding Hagen.

"Hagen!" Holly's squeal of joy reverberated in his eardrums and he watched as she launched herself at her sister.

Haley stood, mouth open, shock on her face before she too was throwing herself at Hagen, before turning to him, standing for a moment, uncertainty on her face before he simply held out an arm and she threw herself at him, her arms tight around him, tears wetting his shirt.

"Brandon! You're home! I didn't think you would ever come home!" Holly stood watching, before she too moved into his hug.

"I am, girls, but we need to talk, and I mean really talk. But first, go get cleaned up and changed. I was about to grill but I'm not sure if I should. Maybe no supper tonight?"

The twins joint squeal of "Brandon" echoed through the kitchen before they took off on a run, their happy voices drifting back to the couple in the kitchen.

Hagen leaned against him, reaching up for his kiss.

"You made them happy. They always wanted a brother."

"I never had any brothers or sisters. They're great. For what it matters, I worry too much about something happening to them."

"Me, too." Hagen moved away from him, her hands reaching for the meat to hand to him and then reaching for the vegetables. "Brandon?"

Brandon paused from walking through the doorway, to turn back, a puzzled look on his face.

"What if we don't catch them in time, and we lose one of the girls or each other? How do we go on?" Hagen refused to look around, not wanting to see shock and condemnation on his face.

Brandon was back across the room, the meat dropped on the table as he gathered Hagen close to his heart.

"I pray that doesn't happen. We don't know what God has planned, but we will go on, serving Him, following the dreams He has given us. My dream is a long life with my lady." He kissed her thoroughly, leaned back to study the face of the woman he adored, and then turned back to pick up the meat and head for the balcony and the grill, a whistle trailing behind him, warming her heart.

Hearing a tap at the door, Hagen headed that way, giving Haley the plate of vegetables to take out to Brandon and asking Holly to dig out the plates and flatware. She stood on tiptop to peek out, her one hand flat on the door, the other hand on the lock. She twisted the lock and stepped backwards as she opened the door.

"Daniel?" She peeked out, not seeing anyone. "How did you get here?"

"Let's see. Baird, Brady, Brennen and Burnie paid me a visit and made me an offer I couldn't refuse." He handed her a box, a grin on his face. "This is what I found. The fellows were really interested in it. Burnie kept asking if he could look, it might be a bestselling novel in the box."

Hagen began to laugh, picturing Burnie doing just that. "He would, wouldn't he? Maybe, just maybe, I'll let him take a peek." She set the box down in the kitchen and then pointed through the living room. "Brandon and the girls are out there. Head on out. I just have to grab some rolls and the condiments." She reached for an extra plate and flatware and stepped back as Daniel grabbed up the tray.

"Lead the way, milady. Let's find that fellow of yours."

Hagen finally stood, flushed with laughter, to gather the remnants of their meal, the twins reaching for what she had in her hands, pointing back to her seat. Shaking her head, Hagen headed into the apartment, her hands resting for a moment on the box, before the twins approached, a tray of fresh coffee and juice and a plate of cookies in Haley's hands.

"What's that, Hagen?" Holly touched the box.

"It's from Dad's safe. Daniel emptied it for me. I need, rather, we need to go through it. I think there might be something in there but I can't be sure."

"Did Dad have a safety deposit box?" Holly looked uncertain as she asked.

"He did. I cleaned it out when I was settling the estate. There was only some old mortgage information on the house. I handed it over to the lawyer, who has it in his safe."

Hagen seated herself, her hands resting on her lap, her eyes on Brandon, who nodded.

"Daniel, we need to bathe this with prayer. Will you lead?"

Chapter 39

Her hands shaking, a prayer on her lips, Hagen reached into the box, pulling out the papers and then setting the box aside, Brandon reaching for it and setting it on the table behind him. He watched her carefully, ready to step in if he had to.

"Hagen? What is there?" Holly and Haley had moved from their seats to stand beside her, the two men moving so the twins could sit beside her.

"I don't know." Hagen paused for a moment. "I don't know what we'll find, Haley, Holly. I really don't. Dad never said much, only told me if something happened to him, I would have to deal with it."

She sighed, reaching for the first piece of paper and unfolding it. "This is just tax information that I have dealt with." She looked around, finding Brandon heading back outside with a pile of blank folders, labels, and pens in his hands.

"Here, girls. You can label the folders as Hagen decides what each piece of paper is. If you can, sort it by date or by alphabet, depending on what there is."

Hagen moved rapidly after that, sorting through the material with the girls' help until she reached the very last piece of paper, a sealed envelope with her name on it, written in her father's handwriting. She paused, her finger tracing the writing, blinking back tears before she loosened the flap and opened the large brown envelope.

"What is that?" Holly's finger touched the documents.

"I'm not sure, Holly. Let's see what Dad left. A passport, but it's not his photo or name. A list of phone numbers with only initials. Photos of? That's Billy and Ben, isn't it, Daniel?"

Daniel reached for it, Brandon leaning over to look. "It is, I would say about 10 years ago. Around the time, I think that you landed here, Brandon, or just before."

"About that time. I transferred in to finish my degree, I had about 18 months left." He reached for the photo. "Is this the old farm?"

"Not that one. This is another one." Daniel sat back before he looked at him. "I wonder if there's another jail cell."

Brandon sat back, shocked. "I wonder. We'll let Dallas worry about that, shall we? Hagen? What else do you have there?"

Hagen looked up, her face drawn and white. "This. A letter written by Dad, or almost a journal, detailing the crime the Richards had been up to. He states he was afraid for his life and for Mom and us." She heard the intake of breath from the twins. "Brandon, what if their accident wasn't an accident? What if it was deliberate?"

"How? Wasn't it a drunk driver?" Brandon was puzzled, his eyes on her face, trying to understand where she was heading with her questions.

"That driver was notorious for being able to drink a lot and not seem drunk. He was often stopped and blew well over the limit. In fact, at the time, he didn't have a driver's license." Daniel shared a look with Hagen. "Unfortunately, I can see the Richards setting him up and having him play chicken with your parents, Hagen. Only he was too drunk to have the proper reflexes."

"And then his family found out, began to blackmail the Richards, and they decided to set me up for revenge." Hagen was on her feet, anger driving her to pace, before she swept the material back into the envelope. "Are the guys in the conference room, Brandon?"

"I think they planned to be." He squinted at his watch in the dimming light. "They should still be. Girls, how be you and Daniel clean up and then head on down there? We could use your insights."

"You can? I mean, you want us to help?" Haley was incredulous.

"We didn't think you did. So we never offered." Holly was on her feet, almost running for the kitchen.

"We have been remiss, I think, my love." Brandon's hand reached for Hagen's. "They may have the insight we've been lacking."

"They have good imaginations. Will that help?" Daniel grinned at the couple, before he headed in to help the girls, finding them almost finished. "What? You didn't wait for me?"

They turned before they began laughing, teasing him with the ease of old friends.

Brandon stood for a moment outside the conference room door, his hand on Hagen's cheek.

"When we go through here, and give them this, and ask for help, there will be no going back."

Hagen nodded, her hand coming up to grip his. "I know, my love. But we need to do this. We need this over. We can't go on with our dream of making my work your work in a more educational, teaching way."

Chapter 40

Standing just inside the door, Hagen and Brandon watched the beehive of activity, as he termed it later on, going on in the room, all thirteen men there, the wives, Farr and Alice, Eric, Fynn's cousin and his wife, Sandra, and Will. That shouldn't have surprised them, but it did.

"I thought Will was on holidays." Hagen's whisper to Brandon, though quiet, seemed to echo through the room, raising heads and then with glad cries, raising the occupants to their feet, to come and greet Brandon and herself.

Daniel, Haley and Holly slipped quietly inside, heading for seats near Will, dropping into quiet conversation with him.

"Brandon? You're okay?" Barnabas stood beside him, his hand on his friend's shoulder.

"I am, Barnabas. I wasn't harmed, which is the strange part of it all. Just held in a jail cell, set up just for me."

"A jail cell?" Burnie exchanged a glance with the others. "Arranged just for you? That's bizarre."

"Not if you know the people involved." Hagen spoke quickly. She held up the envelope. "I have information here that I didn't know Dad had. I hadn't looked in the safe since they were killed. I'm sorry."

She blinked back tears before heading towards her sisters.

"Sorry? For what?" Benen watched her walk away with the ladies in the room heading after her.

"Her father named the Richards. He had dates, a list of initials, a passport that we don't know who it belongs to, an almost diary of facts and details about them. She feels guilty, that if she had found it, perhaps none of this would have happened."

"God's timing, Brandon." Buckley spoke quietly before he headed towards Hagen, a hand on her arm drawing her to one side. They could see him speaking with her before their heads bowed and the men know Buckley was praying with and for her.

"It's all in here." Brandon handed it off to Brody. "Make us copies and then hand the originals to Will. He needs to have this. I think that it will likely aid in other investigations they have on the go."

The men scattered, back to what they had been on, quiet conversation mingling with the click of keys and the rustle of paper. Haley and Holly had finally given in, and headed for bed, Daniel walking them up before he returned, a thought crossing his mind.

He approached Breck, who was free for a moment, standing staring down at the coffee pot.

"It won't pour itself into your cup, Breck." Daniel grinned as Breck looked up, shaking his head to clear it.

"I know. I'm just puzzled."

"About what?"

"The Richards. There just seems to be something or someone missing."

"I know. I think the same thing, but I can't imagine who it is." Daniel turned as he heard a throat clear near him.

Brady stood there. "Fynn and I have been talking. I think I have a name to suggest. Emma's running it for me." They stared at him when he gave the name before Daniel nodded.

"Perfect sense. That's who is behind them. Now, how do we prove it?"

"With a lot of hard work and searching. Daniel, I'm going to pass that name on to Dallas." Breck walked away, the two men watching him before Brady's eyes strayed to Brandon, seeing the fatigue weighing his friend down. "We need to solve this, Daniel. We can try all we want to encourage him, to keep him motivated and moving forward. That's the mission of the Foundation, to provide encouragement. But if it doesn't resolve soon, he'll lose hope."

"I know and so will Hagen. I can tell you this, after being friends with her all our lives. If she starts to lose hope, she will hide it and hide it well. I'm not sure either myself or the twins would be able to read her well enough to discern that."

"That would be true. What do you think about the person Brady named?"

"High in the government, in exports and imports, customs? Absolutely. There have been rumours around about him and his daughter for years. She runs a customs business, helping businesses and individuals make their way through the customs process. It would be a perfect cover."

"I agree." Brady turned for a moment, finding Hagen standing beside him. "Hagen?"

"Daniel, what name did Brady give you?" She kept her eyes on Brady. When he stated it, she nodded, then help up some papers. "These were in with Dad's stuff. Will needs to have it, but take a look at it first, please."

Hagen watched Brady walk away before she turned to make herself another tea, hesitation in her manner, so unlike her that Daniel frowned.

"Hagen?"

"What if we're wrong, Daniel? What if we accuse the wrong person?"

Brandon's arms surrounded her. "It will go no further than our friends, Will and Dallas. They will verify it either as true or not. Trust them, Hagen. I know that is something that is difficult for you at present."

"It is, Brandon, and it shouldn't be." She leaned her head against his arm, her arms wrapped around his. "I hate this, Brandon. And you're about out on your feet."

"I am, but I want to stay." He frowned as she giggled. "What did I say?" He looked up at the snicker from Brady.

"You sounded like a little kid who was told to go to bed and was refusing." Brady grinned as he walked away. "Listen to your wife, Brandon."

Hagen bit back her own snicker before she pulled Brandon from the room and walked towards the stairs. "He's right. You do need to sleep. Your body needs to recover."

Hours later, Hagen curled up in a corner of the couch, a blanket over her, her cup of tea beside her. She studied the cup, a china cup, she thought, with a picture of her favourite bird, a Baltimore oriole on it. Brandon had sought it out for her, she thought. Thank you, Lord, for him. He has brought so much to my life. I don't feel alone and frightened any more. And he's helping with the girls, stepping in as a brother and also a father figure for them that they need. She turned her head as she heard footsteps and Brandon appeared, reaching to shift her over so he could sit with her and then drew her tight to him.

"Can't sleep?"

She shook her head. "Too much on my mind, I guess." Her head went to his shoulder, even as her hand reached for his. "I didn't mean to wake you."

"You didn't, not really. I hadn't got into a deep sleep. Too much to think about." He tilted his head to study her face. "About that name?"

"Yeah, that name. What if we're wrong?"

"At this point, I don't think we are. Dallas will work his magic, or let God work through him, I should say, to prove or disprove it."

"I know." She reached forward to retrieve her phone from the coffee table. "Nathaniel sent me this. Apparently that group has been working on it as well, along with Emma and her employees. He said that given the name Daniel had mentioned, it is more than likely to be the right one. He had found information on that person, but couldn't connect to us. He thought it was old information. Emma apparently has been tracking this person for years."

"She has? You mean, we're the means to bring this person to justice?"

"It would appear so." Hagen tossed her phone to the table and yawned, turning her face into Brandon's shoulder and sleeping.

Brandon watched her sleep, a cry rising from his heart that God would solve this soon, that she would be safe. He wanted so much to be an encourager for her, but he felt he had failed in that.

Chapter 41

Looking up from his desk as his secretary, Amy, appeared in his office doorway, Barnabas beckoned her in.

"Amy?"

"Amos Thomas is out there, Barnabas. He is insistent that he has to speak with you, and right now." Amy was disturbed, that was easy to see.

"Amos? No, I can't. Not right now. I have that conference call with Dad and the rest of the Board in five minutes."

"I told him that. He is refusing to leave. He scares me today, Barnabas, and that is not easy to do."

"I see." Barnabas pushed back his desk chair, preparatory to rising, when Amy shook her head.

"I called security, and I can hear them now. You stay put. They'll handle him." She walked away, but Barnabas still rose, to stand just inside his office doorway, listening to the loud voice echoing down the corridor before the shutting of the outside office door cut it off.

"Amy?"

"Barnabas, he's gone, but he's vicious today. I have never seen or heard him sound like that. Every." Amy appeared in the hallway, her eyes still on the outside door.

"No, it's not like him. Can you let Breck know and ask him to follow up on it? If he's refused to leave the office, have Breck ask that he be held for questioning and possible trespass charges." Barnabas disappeared back into his office, his mind already on the conference call he needed to be part of.

Amy threw up her hands. "I'll do that, Barnabas. I'll just do that." She jumped as she heard Breck's voice behind her

"You'll just do what?"

"Talk to you. Amos Thomas was just escorted from here. Barnabas wants you to follow up and ask that he be held for possible trespassing charges. The fellows had a hard time getting him to leave."

"I can do that. Listen, is he the one that you mentioned when this all started with Brandon and Hagen?"

"He is. And now look where we are."

"We'll sort it out, Amy. Is Barnabas free?"

Amy shook her head. "No, he has that conference call." She turned to look towards his office. "What's going on with him? There is something more than the guys."

"I know, but he's not talking." Breck hesitated before he shook his head and walked away. There is no way that would be true, he thought.

Opening the conference room door, Dallas looked around, not seeing Brandon or Hagen, but he entered anyway, knowing he had to speak with each of the men and that would take time, time he needed to be spending on other investigations as well. Will had met with him that morning, asked him to concentrate on this case and a couple of others, and let some of the other team members pick up for him in the meanwhile.

Two hours later, Dallas rose, heading for the outdoors, needing to walk for a bit, to digest what he had been told, and to determine how he could fit it in with his own investigation. These guys are great, he thought, and with Emma shooting him so much on the ones that he was investigating, he didn't think it would be long before he could make arrests. But how to keep Brandon and Hagen and the twins safe? That was a question that he didn't know if he had an answer to. He knew Hagen. He knew that she was at her limit and would soon step out of her safe zone and go after the Richards and whoever else it was that she had determined to be involved. She's like her father in that, he thought. When Gallagher and Emily were killed, we lost a power couple in the community. They were both quiet, worked in the background, but they made things happen.

Hagen watched him pacing from the balcony above, before she headed back inside. The twins were home from school already, excited about another few days off, the reason why she just couldn't think of for the moment. Brandon, she knew, was meeting with Breck, looking into a new line of work, but she knew his heart was not in the social work field as it had been, and she blamed the Richards for that. His volunteer work as a mentor to young college students had had to be put on hold for now, he didn't want to risk any harm coming to them, and he missed it, he told her.

———

She sighed, pacing around the kitchen, her arms folded around herself. Now, what was that thought? *Something is niggling at the back of my mind, Lord? Can you help me to remember?*

"Hagen?" She spun as she heard Brandon's voice, a frown on her face as she headed for the hallway, to meet him heading into the kitchen.

"Brandon? You're in a rush."

"I just needed to see you." He wrapped her in his arms, kissing her soundly, before hugging her tight, his head on hers.

"What is going on?" Hagen felt that she could barely breathe, Brandon had her in such a tight hold.

The twins slid to a stop, having heard the excited sounding voices, and frowned at first one another and then at their sister.

"Hagen?"

"I have no idea, Holly. Ask this big oaf, if you must know."

"A big oaf, am I?" Brandon winked at the twins, who had to smother their grins. "Barnabas found Breck and I. He had a meeting this morning with the Board. There is a whole new avenue of work that they want me to look into."

"There is?" At his silence, Hagen pushed back, her eyes narrowed. "And that would be?"

"To work with teens in the courts. There is a need that no one else has tried to meet. Someone from the courts approached the Foundation, and the Board

---

thought of me. It's definitely something that we will need to pray about."

The twins hugged the couple, their hands meeting around them.

"This is so cool, Brandon. You would suit that to a T." Haley watched her sister's face. "Hagen?"

"Sorry, I was wool gathering, I think. This is great news but we need to pray that it is God's will."

"And I talked to Dallas. They are getting ready to arrest the Richards, all five of them, on other charges, but they won't forget about us. Dallas thinks that this will be critical to solving our mystery, or adventure, or whatever you want to call it."

"This is dangerous, right?" Holly stepped back, fear on her face. "It won't end it, will it? When do the people stop following us everywhere we go? We have guys at school trying to trap us into meeting them, into going out with them, into going for pizza with a group."

"Holly? Is that what has been happening?" At her nod, Hagen's eyes slid closed. "How be, for now, I talk to your teachers and see if we can let you work online or at home? Would that help?"

"It would. You worry about us when we're away from you and we worry about you." Haley reached for Hagen, hugging her tighter than she had in years, her fear palpable.

Chapter 42

Benen froze as he read the article on his monitor, sitting back before he printed numerous copies of it. He rose, heading for the printer, grabbing the sheets of paper and tidying them into a neat pile before he sorted them and then stapled each set. He looked around. Not all the guys are here, he thought, noting Brady, Bradon and Buckley were missing. Benen stood for a moment, staring down at what he held, before he walked over to the centre table and cleared his throat, bring all eyes to him, with frowns at the interruption on some faces, frowns that smoothed out as they glimpsed his face.

"Guys, I have an article here that I think we all need to look at. It's not pretty. I don't know how I found it, other than it was God and He knew that we were at a point we needed to see it." He handed around the papers, watching as he saw the moment each man caught the meaning of it.

"Who wrote this?" Burnie was the first to speak.

"I looked into that. She's a lawyer from a town about thirty miles or whatever kilometres away from here. She's been known to walk the line. The law society has been after her, but they had not enough proof."

"Is she the one behind it all?" This from Brody, who had been highlighting sections of the article.

"I would like to think so. She really had it in for Hagen's father, that much is clear from that article. We need to research to see how she would be related to the driver that hit her parents." Benen looked around as he heard footsteps. "Hagen? Brandon?"

"Who were you just speaking about?" Hagen stopped beside Benen, tilting his hand to read the name. "Her? Yes, the driver was her son. Is that the connection? I knew she despised Dad, that he had called her on things on different occasions and had shown her up in court on some cases. She is vindictive, always has been."

"You know her?" Baird moved closer, his eyes on Brandon as he spoke.

"Not personally. Dad made sure that he kept his ladies, as he called us, away from the people he had difficulties with. He didn't like to mix his family life and work life if he could help it. But I remember him talking about her." Hagen had paled. "Did she put her own son up to that, to killing Mom and Dad?" Her hand clamped across her mouth as her stomach roiled. "Who would do that?" Her voice was barely audible.

"Someone who is very sick mentally and emotionally." Brandon wrapped an arm around her. "Have you talked to Dallas?"

"Not yet. He said he would be interviewing the Richards regarding this case today, so he didn't think he'd have time to talk with us." Breck pulled out his phone, his face turning white as he listened, his eyes on Hagen.

———

"Breck?" Hagen was almost afraid to hear what he would have to say.

"Two things, Hagen. Ben Richards died today from a ruptured brain aneurysm that no one knew he had, not even likely himself. Given that, Dallas said Billy has begun to talk, and give names and details that they didn't have yet."

Breck paused, a compassionate look coming over his face. "Your home, Hagen?"

"My home? What about it?" She paled. "They got to it, didn't they?"

"They did. What you didn't know was that Dallas had asked that we clear it out for you, to put everything in storage here. Brandon didn't even know that." He watched as her face moved and then crumpled, tears on her cheeks.

"Thank you. I needed to do that, just wasn't ready to do it myself." She frowned once more. "But that's not all."

"No, it's not. We were finished just after 10. Barnabas had a professional mover go in yesterday and pack everything up, ready for us to go in today." He held up a hand as she went to protest. "We had to move fast, Hagen, in case someone tried when one of you ladies was there. It is a good thing we did. The house exploded about thirty minutes ago."

"Exploded? How? A gas leak?" Hagen searched her mind, trying to comprehend what would have caused the explosion.

"No, not a gas leak, Hagen."

Brandon finally spoke, his shock wearing off. "I think what Breck is trying to say, Hagen, is that someone planted a bomb and blew the house up."

"A bomb?" Her voice rose to a squeak, as she stared around at the men who had gathered closer. "A bomb? Were they trying to kill us?"

"More than likely send a message." Blair spoke up, his hand rubbing at his cheek. "They want you to stay silent and not say anything. Somehow, I don't think that will work."

"No, it won't." They could hear the anger in her voice. "That was our home. I was holding on to it until the girls reached majority. Then, we would have made a decision as to what we all wanted to do with it. They have taken that decision away from us, and they had no right to do that."

"No, they didn't." Breck spoke. "And we will catch them." He tapped the paper he held. "Would she do something like that?"

"Absolutely. We had suspicions that she had done this in the past. People would have their cars explode or burn, or there would be a fire in the home. Arson, but without any proof as to who did it. Not just in this town, either." She looked up at Brandon. "How do I tell the twins?"

"We'll do it together. Buckley will be there, if you like."

She shrugged, before snatching the papers from Breck's hands and stalking away, to slam herself down into a chair, the papers slapped down on the table in

———

front of her, as with pen in hand, she stabbed at the sheets.

"I gather she's a little upset?" Breck stared after her in awe, not quite sure he had really seen what he had just witnessed.

Brandon grinned. "That she would be. Touch her family and she becomes a mother bear. She has had to do that over the last year, to protect the girls but more importantly to protect her heart. She's learning to share that with me."

"Does that mean what we just saw, you'll do?" Burnie spoke up, a smirk on his face.

"You just might. So don't be surprised." Brandon turned back to his friends. "So, how do we go about getting the goods on this woman and giving them to Dallas?"

"For starters, we have a surveillance video from a neighbour's outdoor camera. They had trouble with trespassers and set one up. They called Barnabas and offered it to him, as well as giving a copy to the investigating officer today." Breck paused, not quite sure how to go on.

"Who was it, Breck?" Blair's heart sank, not really wanting to know.

"It was someone who had dressed up as Daniel, but it wasn't him. Burnie and Brody were within him at the time. He was being set up, to cause even more anguish to Hagen."

"I hope they have him hidden away." Brandon could feel the anger beginning to burn in him.

———

213

"He is. Dallas won't say where, and frankly, if we don't know, we can't compromise his safety." Breck reached for another copy of the article. "So, who gets to go see Dallas?"

Chapter 43

A hand to her throat, Hagen stared at the woman standing in front of her, an arm out to shove her sisters behind her. Why was this woman here, in the middle of Hagen's town, in broad daylight, tracking her down and standing in her way?

"Girls, when I give the word, turn and run like you have never run before. We're not that far from the police department. Head there." Hagen continued to back up, shoving her sisters behind her. "Now, run. Send help."

The twins took one last look and then did exactly as she asked, running for the police department, shoving open the door to the shock of the officer on duty, who can out as they called for help. A quick question and he was calling for help, sending the responding officers on their way, his arms encircling the twins and drawing them away from the door, into a sheltered area of the lobby.

Hagen heard the girls' feet pounding on the pavement as they ran, and she thanked God that their parents had drilled into them that they responded instantly when asked to do something in an emergency, not stopping to ask questions or find out the reason why.

"So, you think that will save you and the brats?" Leanne Fuller stared at Hagen, before she shook her head, a taunt on her face. "That won't work. I'll track them down and hold them hostage, to make you do what I want.”

Hagen was puzzled. She knew what Leanne wanted, or at least she thought she did.

“What on earth do you mean? I thought you wanted my business to transport illegal goods.”

Leanne snorted. “That was the Richards’ idea. Not mine. No, I have another plan.” Her words were drawn out, as if she were just coming up with her nefarious plot. “No. Your parents weren’t to have died that night. It was to have been a warning. Only my stupid son had to be drunk.”

“He was drunk all the time, Leanne. Didn’t you know that?” Hagen was still puzzled, trying to read the other woman and unable to.

Leanne’s hand shook as she pulled it from her pocket, a weapon in it. “No, he was not. He was never drunk. Those were all lies about him.” She waved her hand. “Lies your father told and had everybody believing.”

Hagen continued to frown, even as she began to inch backwards, knowing there was a doorway she could slip into if she could only reach it. Just a few more feet. She just had to keep Leanne talking and distracted.

“No? Sorry, Leanne. He did it to himself. Everyone knew how much he liked his alcohol, and his drugs. Did you supply him with those?”

“Of course not. We’re not talking about him. We’re talking about you. I need to kill you, my dear, to exact revenge. Your father thwarted me too many times. I could have been rich and retired except for him.”

“I doubt that, Leanne. Someone would have stepped into your path and stopped you. How close are they to doing just that? Oh, and my house? That was you, wasn’t it. Trying to pass yourself off as Daniel.”

“No, that was Daniel. He’s lied to you all your life.” Leanne had stopped walking, distracted by a sound behind her.

“No, it was you.” Hagen made a lunge for the door, pulling it open and letting it slam behind her, running through the stock room, desperately seeking for a place to hide. She scrambled into a narrow opening, pulling piles of rolled plastic in front of her, and crouching down, her head buried in her arm, one hand across her mouth to silence her gasps for breath. She listened intently, hearing the door slam open against an outside wall and then the clatter of high heels on the concrete floor as Leann entered, searching for her.

“Where are you, you little...!” Leanne’s anger was such that she could not even finish a sentence, her free hand hitting at the boxes and packages on the shelves, not finding Hagen.

Leanne finally stood, close to where Hagen had hidden, before she spun in a circle, off balance, the alcohol she had consumed for courage beginning to work against her. She didn’t realize just how much she had imbibed.

Hearing a sound, she walked as quietly as she could on her high heels towards it, her weapon up. She saw the shadow moving quickly towards her and her weapon discharged. She heard the sound of a surprised cry, frowning as it sounded more male than female, and that couldn't be right, she thought. Leanne stumbled forward, to stand, tottering on her heels, staring down at the crumpled form in front of her, not hearing the running steps heading her way or the jerk as her arms were pulled behind her or feel the cuffs as they closed with a metal snap around her wrists. Her weapon was taken and bagged before she was led away.

Will dropped to his knees, hands outstretched to turn the officer over, his heart clenching as he saw it was Dallas. He looked up to nod at the comment that help was on the way.

Alice stood beside him for a moment, before she looked around.

"Who was she after? It had to be someone."

Will rose, stepping back as other officers moved in to help Dallas, the paramedics almost running their way with the stretcher loaded down with their kits.

"It was Hagen. The twins appeared in the lobby of the building, asking for help. Dallas responded and this is what happened." Will spun. "Hagen had to have come in here. This is close to where the twins said they were."

"Then, she's hidden herself away." Alice gave a grim smile. "We used to do that to one another when we were small, hide and not say a word when the others were looking for us. It was good practice. Only I never expected to have to have Hagen do that as an adult."

"None of us did." Will beckoned to some officers. "Hagen is here. Hiding from what we suspect. Start a search, making sure that she knows we're the good guys."

A soft sound had Will spinning once more, to find Hagen standing behind him, her eyes on him, staring from a white, white face, with fear etching lines on it.

"Will? Alice? Where is she?" Hagen tried to see around him, spotting the body on the floor. "Oh, no! Who is that?"

Alice was beside her, an arm around her. "Leann has been arrested. She will not trouble you any longer. She's facing some stiff charges."

"But who is that?" Hagen's finger shook as she pointed.

"It's Dallas. He was shot by Leanne as he approached this area. It's in his shoulder, so we'll see how severe it is." Will's hand reached to steady her.

"Is it over?" Hagen's voice was barely audible.

"We think so, Hagen." Will gave a gentle smile as he pointed behind her for Alice to walk her out that way, his steps matching theirs, a hand out to steady her if needed. "We'll sort it all out, find out who all she has had dealings with, and then lay the charges."

"She's the one who planted the bomb." Hagen stopped suddenly, swaying as the adrenaline released itself. "I'm tired."

Will gave a quiet laugh. "I have no doubt that you are. Let's get you to the department, get your statement, and then get you and the twins home. Brandon will be waiting for you, no doubt. His friends have been busy, Dallas tells me, his hands apart to show how much material they brought him."

"They're good. They've had practice." Hagen yawned, the only thing holding her upright Alice's arm around her.

Chapter 44

Late that night, Hagen wrapped herself in a blanket and sank gratefully down into her favourite wicker chair on the deck, the china cup of tea beside her. The twins had taken time to settle down, overwrought as they were, but they had finally succumbed to sleep, Hagen watching closely before dropping a kiss on their heads, pulling the covers up tight as she had when they were tiny and she was tasked with putting them to bed, whispered a prayer over each one, and then closing their doors, walked away to find Brandon standing, waiting for her with open arms, to gather her close. His tears wet her hair as her tears wet his sweatshirt, before he prayed for her, whispered some verses in her ear, handed her the blanket and her cup of tea, and told her to go and spend some time with God.

Hagen was grateful for the man she had married, who she loved so deeply, and had so quickly. God had provided just who she needed, she thought. Brandon was the one who had walked through her dreams as a teen, refined as a young adult, but who she had never expected to find. She shifted in her chair to be able to rest her head against the chair back, her eyes on the dark sky, watching the stars in their twinkling and the moon as it sent its rays earthward. It was a favourite time of day for her, a time that she could relax and reflect, to gather her thoughts and her ideas from that day, and to look forward to the next.

She lifted her head as she heard the door open and close and then felt herself lifted up as Brandon scooped her to his heart and then sat back down, cradling her close to him.

"Okay, my love?" His breath whispered across her ear.

"Getting there. It will take time. The twins will need help, I think."

"Buckley thought of that. He has a list of people they can talk to, including a friend of Emma's."

"Darcy, Doug's wife. They had an adventure that almost killed her and almost destroyed the town of Riverville. Revenge from a rogue police chief. Yes, she would be good. A retired forensics psychologist."

"You know interesting people." His chin rested against her head and he was content to hold the lady he loved more than his own life.

"We'll get there. Did you talk to Will? I haven't heard about Dallas. Alice has been tied up with the investigation."

"I did. Dallas is fine, just staying overnight in the hospital for observation. She winged him and when he went down, he hit his head hard. He's fighting mad, Will tells me."

Hagen laughed. "He would be. He always did hate for injustice to win." She snuggled closer. "I never expected this, you know."

"Expected what?" Brandon had no idea of where she was heading with her words.

"You. Me. My shop. Your friends who are now my friends. The ladies. It's so overwhelming what God has provided for us. Darby and the twins are becoming close friends, and I'm glad. He'll look out for them. They need that at times."

"And they're good for him. They put him in his place, Berneen tells me."

Hagen laughed. "That they do." She was silent for a while, her thoughts chaotic until she just gave up trying to sort them out. "Brandon, if we had to choose a verse for us, given what we've gone through, what would you choose? I know we'll be asked, but I just can't seem to settle on one. My mind is too full of puzzles and hurt and sadness, that it seems that I have lost sight of my dreams."

"Never that, darlin'. Never that. Your dreams are there, just waiting to surface. Your Dad and Mom's dreams are there as well, those they chose to share with you. And the twins? They will have their own dreams, some to share, some to keep private even from one another. As to a verse? That's a good question. I might not be able to come up with one tonight."

"That's okay. I just thought we should be looking at something. Dad and Mom chose a verse when they married for them as a couple, even though they each had a life verse."

"I like that idea. I know you have a life verse. So do I." Brandon's voice paused. "I know what we can do. A dream that was my mother's. I had forgotten it. How be we take part of your business, and dedicate it to making plaques or signs with people's life verses? Have them choose a favourite picture or scene and incorporate it into the project?"

"I like how you think. Mom wanted that, but she never pushed, wanting the educational portion to be first. We need to update our website and include that." Hagen shifted again, this time her mind racing with possibilities.

"Turn off the thoughts, my love. Just rest. You've been through a lot. The next few days and weeks will be exhausting for you as you release the stress and strain that you and the twins have been under."

When Hagen didn't answer, Brandon shifted her enough to see her face. He smiled, and then sat back, his own eyes closing as he too slept. It had been an emotional day for them both, and God had granted them what they needed most, sleep.

Three months later, Brandon stood for a moment in the shop door, watching as Hagen concentrated on a project. He walked towards her, a hand resting on her shoulder as she looked up, a smile lighting up her face

"You're home and early!" She was on her feet and in his arms, her face raised for his kiss.

"I am and free until the middle of next week. Barnabas sent me home, told me to go find the lady I loved and spend the days with her. Know who that would be?" He laughed as she playfully swatted his arm. "What are you working on?"

"A new idea. God has been giving me too many dreams and ideas. I start on one and then another and another comes from that." She was glowing and he loved that.

"God is using you in a way I don't think even your father would have imagined. Go with the creative juices. We have been able to hire, through Buckley's contacts, and those men and ladies are happy for the work. You are providing encouragement to them and through them to others. It's snowballing. You are doing exactly what the Foundation envisioned."

"As are you. I talk to the youth that you work with. They hunt me down in town or at church, singing your praises, telling me how much better they feel about themselves because of you." She moved away from him. "I did this today."

"Did what?" He approached her as she stood, staring down at a framed picture, his arm coming around her. "Our verse. As for me and my house, we will serve the Lord. Joshua 24:15. New King James Version. And you chose a picture of your home. That's is nice. I like it." He kissed her again, before staring down at it, frowning as she moved it to one side. "What's this? Hagen?" He stared down at the picture that lay on the table.

"Brandon?"

"Hagen? Is this what I think it is?" He turned her to face him, surprise and awe on his face. "What are you telling me?"

"That I think you'll make a great father. I have seen how you react and teach the twins, not belittling them but building them up even when you have to reproof or correct them."

"When?" He just hugged her tighter and tighter.

"Brandon! I need to breathe!" Hagen's happy laughter spilled out and around the shop. "In about six months more or less. And we need to set up for two. That means the twins have to share."

Brandon stepped back, his hands on her shoulders. "Two? As in twins?" At her nod, he had to reach for a stool and sit. "Twins! Wow!"

Hagen laughed even as she reached for her phone, a frown in place as she saw it was Dallas.

"Dallas? We haven't talked in a week or two. I thought we weren't talking." Hagen could feel Brandon staring at her in shock.

Dallas' laugh carried across through the phone. "I know. I thought that too. I need to meet with you two. Is now a good time?"

"As good as any, I guess. Where?"

"Seeing as I'm standing right outside your shop door, will that work?" She spun as she saw him heading in, tucking his phone away in a pocket, a grin on his face, and then looked past him to see thirteen men and six ladies following in his footsteps.

"What is this? A party I didn't know I was hostess to?" Hagen was grinning as she greeted each one.

"No, we're giving the party and it's for later." Barnabas gave her a hard hug and then shook Brandon's hand. "Dallas asked to meet with us all. He wouldn't tell me why." He grinned at the face Dallas shot him and smirked in response.

Dallas studied each of the ones sitting or standing around, his gaze resting last on Hagen and Brandon, a frown on his face for a moment before he nodded.

"I just needed to update all of you on the investigation. Leanne Fuller has turned around and pled guilty to the charges facing her, including assault on and attempted murder of a police office, namely me. She has faced a slew of charges from this town and numerous towns around. The forces are glad to have her off the street.

"It is as you suspected, Hagen. Revenge. She was plotting revenge on your father, not realizing that the Richards were plotting the same, and using her son in their devious plans. He wasn't to have died, as we thought. He was to have just run them off the road and then disappeared. The Richards had it all worked out to move him from town, change his identity and then forget about him. We suspect they had hired a hit man to get rid of him, but Billy Richards has refused to confirm that.

"It all comes back to what you had found. Your father had information on Leanne that he was ready to turn in. She found out about it and then tried to find it. She is also the one who set the bomb in your home, pretending to be Daniel.

"The Richards had wanted your business to use for smuggling contraband, namely jewels and drugs. They had planned to frame you if anything was found. They were the ones who set your original shop on fire, as a warning, only it took a much bigger hold than they planned. Not the brightest ones, those five. Yes, all five were involved.

"Ben is the one on the dirt bike. He had it planned, where you had your tent, that Brandon would meet you, that you would step away and talk. He knew you would do just that. He had arranged for the floor joist to be almost cut all the way through in strategic spots, likely doing it himself. He's the one who had your sister kidnapped.

"Now, let's see. I think that covers it all. Any questions?"

Hagen's voice could be heard softly in the quiet that followed Dallas question. "I do not need to avenge. God will avenge. In so much better a way for us." She looked up at Brandon, who nodded, before she rose and went to each individual with a hug and a thank you.

Brandon stood for a moment, his eyes on his friends, knowing that he and Hagen had not faced what the six of them had.

"I can't find the words, guys, ladies, to thank you. You have been what true friends are. Thank you, each one of you." His hands rested on Hagen's shoulders. "Hagen has been busy. I know she has found out what verse is important to you and what kind of scenery you like the best. In those boxes sitting by Buckley's left arm, you will find a framed photo, with your verse on it, as a small thank you from Hagen, Haley, Holly and myself."

There was silence before laughter and talk broke out, the boxes distributed and each one standing in amazement at the artwork that Hagen had prepared, awed at her ability to choose a photo that so encompassed their dreams

Dear Readers

Thank you once more for picking up one of my books, this time the story of Brandon and his lady, Hagen. Once more these two characters have taken me on a windy, twisty road of adventure, not letting me see the road map in advance. Hagen's name was not originally Hagen. She chose this one. The twins, Haley and Holly? Not planned at all. In fact, I had no idea she has not an only child until they just showed up and in my thoughts enhanced the story and added a bit of fun to it.

My dream since a child was only known to my Mom and that only a couple of years before she graduated to heaven in 2010. The dream? To write a novel. That novel, *The Sparrow*, started off a three year so far adventure of meeting characters and telling their stories, usually with the author not having a clue what was to happen, and with their unruliness, a chance to explore occupations and what not that I normally would not have done.

God knew my dream. He let it sit for probably fifty years before I set hands to the keyboard and wrote that novel. He knows your dreams. He knows when the timing is right. He knows who you need to reach and why. Trust Him with those dreams. Wait on His leading and timing. He'll guide you through the process.

The verse from Joshua? My father chose that when he and my mother married, for it to be the verse for their home. It has special meaning to me because of that. Isn't that what we, as believers, are to do? Serve the Lord and with gladness.

God bless each one of you. May He grant you the fulfillment of your dreams.

Ronna